FIRST CLASS TICKET

FIRST CLASS TICKET

—A NOVEL—

Ann Marie Zakos

Magnum Veritas Publishing
ELK GROVE VILLAGE, ILLINOIS

© 2006 Ann Marie Zakos.
Printed and bound in the United States of America.
All rights reserved. No part of this book may be reproduced or transmitted
in any form or by any means, electronic or mechanical, including photocopying,
recording, or by an information storage and retrieval system—except by a reviewer who
may quote brief passages in a review to be printed in a magazine, newspaper, or on the
Web—without permission in writing from the publisher. For information, please contact
Magnum Veritas Publishing, P.O. Box 355, Elk Grove Village, IL 60009.

This book is a work of fiction. Names, characters, places, and events
are products of the author's imagination or are used fictitiously. Any resemblance to actual
events, locations, or persons, living or deceased, is purely coincidental. We assume no
responsibility for errors, inaccuracies, omissions, or any inconsistency herein.

First printing 2006

ISBN-13: 978-0-9764523-3-1
ISBN-10: 0-9764523-3-2

LCCN 2004118027

ATTENTION CORPORATIONS, UNIVERSITIES, COLLEGES,
AND PROFESSIONAL ORGANIZATIONS: Quantity discounts are available on bulk
purchases of this book for educational, gift purposes, or as premiums for increasing
magazine subscriptions or renewals. Special books or book excerpts can also be created
to fit specific needs. For information, please contact Magnum Veritas Publishing,
P.O. Box 355, Elk Grove Village, IL 60009; (866) 766-7404.

www.annmariezakos.com

TABLE OF CONTENTS

Acknowledgments   **vii**

Preface   ix

Chapter I   A Rare Coincidence   1

Chapter II   Philosophy 231   8

Chapter III   Perceptions and Misconceptions   15

Chapter IV   Forces of Nature   27

Chapter V   Mask of the Ego   40

Chapter VI   Misunderstood Truth   51

Chapter VII   The Third Eye   71

Chapter VIII   The Core   85

Chapter IX   The Key of Love   105

Chapter X   Body of Earth   120

Chapter XI   Keystone, True, and Jeremiah   134

Chapter XII   On the Strings of Violins   149

Chapter XIII   A Deeper Assignment   160

ACKNOWLEDGMENTS

Words cannot express how thankful I am to the special people in my life that have helped me with this project. I would like to extend my warmest love and gratitude to my family. To my parents Dan and Toula Zakos, sister Angela, brother Pete, and sister Niki, thank you for shaping me into the person that I am. I love you very much.

I would like to thank everyone at About Books for understanding my vision and making it a reality. Your knowledge, expertise, and incredible support have helped me tremendously. Thank you to Scott and Debi Flora, Sue Collier, Cathy Bowman, Kate Deubert, Deb Ellis, Cindy Crosby and Allan Burns. Thanks for all your hard work. Also a very special thank you goes to Patrick Norton for your encouragement and inspiration throughout this entire project.

Lastly, I would like to thank you, the reader, for reading my words and understanding the profound message that I had to share with you all. You deserve a book like this, and it is with great love that I deliver it to you. May you all be blessed through your own personal adventure.

*The nation cannot afford to be
materially rich and spiritually poor.*
—John F. Kennedy

PREFACE

The events of September 11 and the war in the Middle East have inspired a spiritual awakening. Now, more than ever, people are turning to their inner spirituality to determine the meaning of life. It is apparent that the dawning of the new millennium has aroused a shift in our worldview as our culture undergoes a cognitive reformation. But there are so many questions still left unanswered. What are we doing here? What is life all about?

If you find yourself reading this book, perhaps it is time to gain a better understanding of who you are. It is time to stop searching and time to start believing that everything you want in life can be fulfilled. You just have to recognize where to find it.

We are all trying to experience "something," trying to feel "something," trying to love "something." And it is that "something" that is supposed to validate who we are. It is that "something" that is supposed to make us complete. But what happens when that "something" doesn't come? We start searching all over again.

In 2006, many of us are still searching for that "something." This constant searching is the reason for the unhappiness, because in our quest for finding that "something" we feel as if we have failed. Sure, we might experience short spurts of happiness but what happens when those feelings dissipate? We start searching again. We start looking to the exterior for that "something." The truth is that "something" has always been inside of us but we have failed to recognize it. We have failed to fully grasp it. The fulfillment and the joy we are looking for is within us.

This fictional journey explains how to find that "something," and it clarifies how to tap into the love, happiness, and success of which we have always dreamed. The new understanding starts here.

*Not everything that can be counted counts, and not
everything that counts can be counted.*

—Albert Einstein

I

A RARE COINCIDENCE

I didn't want to do it. I had no desire to. I thought everything was set, solid, and secure. What does that advisor…counselor—or whatever she calls herself—know about anything? She told me I didn't have to take another elective class. I can't be up at the crack of dawn. I'm poky as hell in the morning, and anyway I had my journalism classes to worry about.

Deep thunderous sighs echoed through my college apartment, as my heart sank like the *Titanic* into an angry sea. *Why do I have to do this now?* I turned to find the only thing in the room that I loved: my old ragged couch. In that couch, I found many treasures. I once came across three dollars in change to pay for my week's laundry. But the greatest gift I found was silence. I took deep breaths, the kind the doctor tells you to take when you're on the examining table and he puts that cold stethoscope on your back. I wanted to cleanse my mind of its chaos so I turned on the TV. As I watched with a cloudy head, the sports announcers were ranting and raving about the baseball season. My stomach did somersaults as they spoke. Ugh…philosophy; also known as petty nonsense about one's inner self and the meaning of life. It's interesting to the tree-hugging, hippie-bohemian types. But I wasn't one of them. *Why do I have to take this philosophy class now?* I wanted to scream at the top of my lungs, pull my hair out, and bite my nails down to the cuticles.

Then the sports announcer said the only words that actually registered. *It's time for the wamma jamma.* I suddenly sat up and thought about that strange phrase for a second. The wamma jamma? Hmm. Then the show cut to the highlight reel of spectacular plays of the week.

I turned off the television. Half dizzy and half numb, I looked around the room. I heard the tick-tock, tick-tock of the ugly clock Victoria had put on the wall. Like a ticking time bomb, the second hand of the clock pulsed in unison with my anxious heartbeat. Its loud ticking pierced my soul. The ticking grew louder and louder until it devoured the entire room. I felt as though it was going to swallow me. I picked up a pair of rolled-up socks from the laundry basket near my feet and heaved it at the source of evil. *Bam!* I nailed it. I watched in delight as the clock fell from the wall and crashed to the floor making a horrible clunk. I walked over to the beaten clock. Hovering over it with a sinister grin, I glared at it. But still I heard ticking. The second hand kept moving into the dreaded future. The clock read 7:42 A.M.

I swung my book bag over my shoulder, unbolted the heavy wood door, turned the door handle swiftly, and mustered the courage to open the only thing that was protecting me from the inevitable. The door squeaked as it opened. I glanced at the clock lying on the floor. Tick-tock, tick-tock. What did time have in store for me? Why did I have to take this class now? In a huff, I slammed the door behind me as a strange feeling coursed through my body. I brushed the long brown hair from my eyes and fussed with my watch. Its tight leather band was like an octopus' tentacle choking my wrist. My heart was thumping like the second hand of the clock. I wiped my sweaty palms on my new capri pants and staggered into the world.

"Oh…my…God! Madison, is that you?" Just hearing that voice made me cringe. I cleared the frog out of my throat and took another deep breath. My eyeballs rolled into the back of my head. *Should I respond? Or pretend I don't hear her?* I turned my head in slow motion.

"I haven't seen you since last semester. How've you been? Cute bag, where did you get it? Did you grow your hair long? I swear you look taller. I like your French manicure—where did you get it done? Did you lose weight?" *Oh great, why me? As if my morning hasn't been bad enough I have to run into the Plague of all people.* That's what we called her. Her real name was Rachel Gibson. Of course she was the only person unaware of her nickname. She always thought we were friends, but I wanted to punch her lights out every time I saw her. Rachel was one of those pretentious sorority types whose main priority in life was to marry rich.

Standing there with her Tiffany's bracelet and dressed in her "Needless Mark-Up" outfit, her large lips moved swiftly over freshly bleached teeth. She was a babbling Barbie doll.

"I'm doing great, Rachel. How are you?" I spoke with half a smile trying not to grit my teeth.

"Oh my God, did you hear I'm dating Jeff Greenberg? You know—the star pitcher on our baseball team? He's loaded." She said it in a whisper but it was still loud enough to turn heads. "Jewish," she said in another whisper. "Trust fund." She limp-wristed her hand and showed me a sparkling rock on her finger. It was obnoxious. "It's not an engagement ring—yet. It's a promise ring. Two karats. Can you believe he bought this for me?"

What was he promising? I wondered. *Not to choke her in the middle of the night?* She batted her black eyelashes at the shiny carbon on her skinny finger. She gawked at it, making love to it in her twisted mind.

"That's great, Rachel. Congratulations! I'd love to stay and chat, but I have to get to class. I can't be late." She looked at me intensely, dying to catch a glimpse of jealousy or an ounce of envy. But I wasn't green. I gave her nothing. I didn't feel she was worthy.

"Okay, okay, run along," she said. "But hey, I know what a sports fan you are so you *have-to have-to have-to* see one of Jeff's baseball games. He's pitching this Sunday and it's a very big game against our rival. There's going to be a lot of pro scouts watching him. He needs all the support. Will you come? Please…please…and then we'll go out and party after."

"I…uh…I'll let you know…I…um might have some other plans on Sunday." Damn. I wanted to tell her to get a life, to get lost. *Look, I don't like you,* I thought. *You're frickin' annoying, and I don't care about the game or your plans or your stupid, vacant nonsense.* I gritted my teeth trying not to clench my fists.

"Oh, c'mon, it'll be fun, Maddie." My body stiffened and my neck wrenched. I hated being called Maddie—it made the little hairs on the back of my neck stand up like a porcupine. My fists clinched behind my back and I flashed a fake smile. The Plague kept on babbling. She had diarrhea of the mouth and she needed a diaper.

"It's going to be a real exciting game. Plus, you can check out all the cute ballplayers in their tight pants. There are some real hotties on the team…" She sang those words while looking at me coyly and tilted her empty head to the right. She was searching my face for a raised eyebrow. But again, I was stingy.

"So what do you think?" She was singing the words in a higher pitch. *I'm thinking that you have no substance, you silly, silly girl.* That's what I wanted to say. She paused and looked long and hard into my face. Then she said, "You know it's time for the wamma jamma."

I was silent as my jaw hung on its hinges. *What? Huh? The wamma jamma?* I couldn't believe she said those words to me. I had never heard that expression before and suddenly I heard it twice in ten minutes. I looked at her wide-eyed. What was going on?

"Will you come to the game?"

"I'll…I'll…let you know." I turned my head and walked away briskly.

"Call me!" she shouted at my back. I knew I would run into someone, but why of all people did I have to run into the Plague before my first class of the semester? It seemed like a jinx. I had to breathe in the fresh air and rid myself of her venomous infiltration. It was too early to vomit.

Oh, come on, she can't be that bad. That's what I used to say to everyone. But she really was that aggravating. I always recognized coincidences. But what does this coincidence mean? What did our meeting symbolize? What was the wamma jamma? Should I have socialized with her more? I just couldn't do it. Should I go to the game? I didn't have the energy or the desire to talk to her more, but maybe that's the wise thing to do. *Why do I have this gut feeling to go to the game? Oh, what the hell? It might be fun if I don't punch her in the process.*

Coincidences happen. I had a feeling I would see someone. What were those strange words? Wamma jamma. What did she have to tell me? I thought about it more as I walked toward my philosophy class. I needed to focus on something else. I took deep breaths, filling my lungs with the clean crisp air. I felt more energized. I stared at the tall trees and beautiful landscape around me. The campus looked gorgeous in the morning, but I wouldn't have known that before today. I always tried to schedule my classes 10:30 A.M. at the earliest. My newfound appreciation for the campus seemed to put my mind at ease. I felt stronger. And then my thought process suddenly changed to another strange coincidence that happened last summer.

It was late July, and I was still unsure about my living situation for this school year. I couldn't deal with another year in the smelly dorms, and I was desperately trying to find an apartment that my roommate Victoria and I could live in. I had a strong vision of what I wanted in an apartment. It had to be close to school, and it had to be big and spacious with plenty of room. I looked at a dozen apartments but none of them fit my vision. They were either too small, too musty, too vintage, no dishwasher, walls falling apart, paint chipping, rust in the bathtub, or just too damn filthy. One of them even had a termite problem, not to mention a shower with mildew three inches thick, and a toilet with watermarks as yellow as the putrid urine splashing on the adjacent wallpaper. (Some guys don't have good aim. Is it that difficult to get it in the toilet?)

I didn't have any luck and was becoming really stressed out. The summer was nearly over and I still hadn't found a place. If I didn't find a suitable apartment I would have to commute from home and I didn't want to do that. After seeing tons of apartments I didn't like, I made an appointment with a landlord for one last chance to find a suitable place. The night before I was to see the apartment I had the most coincidental dream.

In the dream it was a blistering hot summer afternoon. I was wearing jean shorts and a white tee shirt. The sun was shining on my face as I stood on the front porch of an old three-flat Victorian apartment building. A small middle-aged man with gray shaggy hair drove up to the building in a blue minivan and attempted to parallel park in a very tight spot. I had never seen the man in the minivan before, but I knew he was the landlord.

The next afternoon was blistering hot. I was wearing jean shorts and a white tee shirt. The sun was shining on my face as I stood on the front porch of an old three-flat Victorian apartment building. A small middle-aged man with gray shaggy hair drove up to the building in a blue minivan and attempted to parallel park in a very tight spot. I had never seen the man in the minivan before, but I knew he was the landlord. It was exactly the same situation I had seen in my dream the night before.

At that moment, I knew the apartment was destined to be mine. It turned out to be everything that I was looking for. It was perfect. It had plenty of room and tall airy ceilings. And it was clean.

When I left the apartment this morning, I had the feeling something was weird. You know how it is when you walk into a grocery store to grab a few things and you're looking like complete dog shit. You have on no makeup, your hair is greasy, and there is a ketchup stain on your shirt. And that is the time you're destined to run into someone you know. You have to pretend you're excited to see them, when in fact, you really want to hide. But, of course, you have to do the petty small talk bit. You have to ask yourself, why did I happen to run into that person in the first place? Was there some particular reason for it?

Then what tops it off is you go home and realize that apart from how completely terrible you looked, you had a piece of spinach stuck between your two front teeth from the chicken Florentine you ate for dinner. Nice. But whatever—those things happen.

Weird things happen to me all the time. Especially in the worst place possible, such as church. Imagine standing up to hear to the reading of the gospel and all of a sudden you feel a rush of something warm and gushy between your legs. You squirm in your Sunday hose and in the midst of your prayers for humanity you realize that you got an unexpected visit from Aunt Flo.

Flo is very happy to see you. She loves to drop by unannounced. You think you have at least another couple days before you have to shake hands with her again. But to show her appreciation for how much she loves visiting you every twenty-eight days she leaves a beautiful red Picasso, a masterpiece if you will, right on the back of your new spring suit. That red display of femininity on your ass is the least good ol' Flo could do. And it's a beauty. A real Picasso.

By the way, I'm Madison Phillips. The next best thing, whatever that means. I'll be watching for the wamma jamma.

*I have never let my schooling
interfere with my education.*

—Mark Twain

II

PHILOSOPHY 231

I finally arrived at philosophy class, which was being held outside in the middle of the campus mall. My pits were sweaty and my mouth dry as I sat down on the lawn and looked around like a lost puppy. I tried to think of something pleasant. At least it was reassuring to know I had a clean slate and a fresh start. I could forget about that C that was like a nasty blemish on my record last semester and focus on my new classes. What is past is past. I had a few minutes to kill, so I decided to do a little people watching before philosophy class started. I thought about how weird it was that the only words I comprehended from the TV this morning were the only two words I got from the Plague. Wamma jamma.

My eyes focused to a girl nobody noticed. Her dark clothing hung on skin and bone. She walked lazily. Gravity pulled down her chin and weighed down her faded cheeks as her eyelids blinked slowly. She didn't notice the other students, nor they her. As she moped, the sidewalk wallowed in her misery.

She looked like a zombie. I watched as her boot quickly suffocated the breathing grass below her feet and stomped on its energy. Like a walking hanger blowing in the wind she trudged across the beautiful field as other students gathered around. Amidst the lavish lawn and huge oak trees she plopped down on the grass and gawked at her hangnails, biting and spitting them into the grass.

In the distance a young man walked briskly toward the other students. With a bounce in his step and a glowing face he gazed appreciatively at the enchanting grassy knoll. His curly brown hair was alive and vibrant and his rugged athletic build conveyed a healthy radiance. His azure eyes sparkled in the sunlight as two dimples appeared on his cheeks. He looked to be searching for recognizable faces, but his exploration found nothing but a group of strangers. He perched himself next to the mopey girl. He reached for an apple in his bag and bit into it with a crunch. The juices from the apple sprayed the air and then slowly dribbled down his chin. He chewed with a smile on his face. He was eager for class to begin. Face down, the mopey girl focused on her hangnails.

I people-watched for a good five minutes. It was an interesting experience, but all based on judgments that aren't necessarily true or valid. I mean, who really knows what someone is based on their physical appearance? These students may not look like people I'd be friends with, but that didn't mean I shouldn't talk to them. I would probably learn more from someone who wasn't like me at all. I wondered why the professor wanted to meet outside instead of in the typical boring classroom with a brown linoleum floor, green chalkboards, and wood desks. The classroom always had a stench of mildew. Whatever the reason, it was refreshing to be outside. I took a notebook and pen out of my leather book bag, unsure of what to expect next. I sat quietly, in anticipation of a new class.

Arriving in front of the students was Dr. Jacobs. His gray wooly beard made a wreath around his face. He was a refined scholar whose presence radiated calmness and assurance in a nerdy yet sexy Sean Connery way. Then I started imagining Sean Connery on top of me, kissing me and caressing my body. I always get distracted with perverted thoughts. I can't help it. With the glare of the sun at his back and the wind whistling through the oak trees, the professor focused on the students still scurrying to find a pleasing seat in the dancing grass.

With a confident nod he addressed the class of fifty students. He began, "Hello, everyone. I am Dr. Jacobs and this is philosophy 231. Consider this class your wake-up call. If you've just been going through the motions of life, you'll soon think again.

"You're probably wondering why we are meeting outside. This will be discussed in our next meeting. The purpose of this class is to discover your truth and to help you follow your truth. You will have the opportunity to have many life-altering experiences during the course of this class, but it's all up to you. Experiences are neutral encounters. You chose to let them affect you positively or negatively. It's your call."

He paused, took a deep breath, and proceeded. "I am passing around the attendance sheet. Along with that please take an envelope but do not open it." The mopey girl looked up from her hangnails as the other students mumbled words under their breath. The glowing boy chewed his apple with delight as the attendance sheet moved around slowly. Students broke into conversations and joked with each other. When the envelopes came around, each student took one as if there were an infectious disease inside. They were shaking the envelopes and rattling them around like it was Christmas morning. Dr. Jacobs waited patiently in silence until every student held an envelope in his or her hand.

"Do you all have an envelope?" Jacobs asked us with a grin. I held the manila envelope with a sweaty grip. I squirmed in the grass and fidgeted with my long hair. What could possibly be inside? What was this all about? I looked at Dr. Jacobs' heavy beard. The sun behind him was like a ball of white light radiating through his entire being. He was starting to look like a prophet.

"Now," he announced, "you have your first-class ticket." The class let out a huge…huh? Ticket? Jacobs proceeded.

"This ticket is your ticket to seeing the world in a whole new way— a magical way. Each ticket inside the envelope contains a written truth. Once you discover these truths, your lives will begin their metamorphosis. This is your lucky day, because inside this envelope is the ticket to who you really are. Consider that you are holding the key to life in your hands." I gazed down at the manila envelope in my sweaty palms. In my hands the envelope was alive.

Dr. Jacobs spoke loudly. "I want you all to look at the person sitting next to you. They must be someone you do not know." The glowing boy glanced at the mopey girl as she timidly looked up from her hands.

Dr. Jacobs' voice projected. "This person will be your experience partner." The boy curiously looked into her bloodshot eyes. "Believe me this is no accident; together you will unravel nine truths. Each ticket inside the envelope has a written sentence on it. Each sentence is a truth. It is your assignment to unravel each truth inside this envelope." Fifty students let out a groan. They began whispering words of discontent as they nervously looked at one another. I couldn't take my eyes off the envelope. I was immersed in it. Suddenly a tall student with shaggy hair blurted out. "What kind of truths? What do you mean?"

"You'll find out," Dr. Jacobs said with confidence.

The class was in an uproar. "What kind of experience partner? What are we supposed to experience together?"

Dr. Jacobs smiled calmly. "Together you will unravel the nine truths of life."

A girl with a high-pitched voice asked, "What kind of truths? I don't get it."

"In these envelopes are nine written truths. They will at first appear to you as vague sentences but these nine statements will grow into extraordinary discoveries for you."

"What? How?" another girl asked.

Dr. Jacobs smiled, "It's okay that it doesn't make sense to you right now. On the back of each ticket is a name of a person on campus. These people will serve as your guides in helping you achieve your new understanding." The class exhaled in relief. "However, you may not contact them directly and you cannot contact me; somehow your guides will find you."

A worried boy stood to his feet. "This is crazy, man. What are you smoking?"

Dr. Jacobs looked at him somberly. "I realize this is something that you've never done before but you must trust the process." Jacobs was calm and peaceful. "Think about it: Everything in your life up to this point has worked out for the better, one way or another. This too will work but you must be open to it." The student's rumbling uncertainty continued. "Since we only meet once a week you should understand these truths by our next meeting, which is a week from today. By that time you should be prepared to relive the experiences that you had. The duration of the course will consist of how to reiterate these truths into your daily lives. By then your mentality will have evolved into a new realm and will proceed to change and grow but you must be able to recognize this metamorphosis."

An angry-looking student interrupted. "Recognize what?" The boy's voice intensified. "You're not going to tell us, right?"

"Just trust your synchronicity."

The class was baffled.

"Who doesn't have a partner?" Dr. Jacobs asked. I abruptly raised my hand high in the air. Dr. Jacobs immediately pointed toward me. "You can be paired up with the guy and gal closest to you." I smiled at them. The glowing boy returned the smile but the mopey girl hardly glanced my way. *What the hell's with her?*

Dr. Jacobs collected his belongings. "I'll meet you next week, same time, same place." He walked into the glare of the sun and meandered off into the beautiful landscape as it engulfed him. The glowing boy glanced at the mopey girl as she looked at him blankly. He beamed and commented, "This sounds really exciting doesn't it?" He held out his hand. "I'm Brian Livingston."

Surprised, she shook his hand weakly. "I'm Diana Forsythe," she mumbled in a low tone.

"I'm Madison Phillips." I politely put out my hand hoping to get a response from her. But nothing.

"So what do you think about this?" Brian mused.

Diana hesitated, then said, "I'm confused, but I'm always confused," as she turned her head away.

"Well…so am I, but I think this could be pretty cool," Brian said.

"I think this sounds very exciting, very different," I said, "but I'm not sure what's expected of us."

Diana's eyes suddenly grew wild. "I don't know, it sounds like bullshit. I think I might have to drop the class."

Brian and I looked at her curiously, then Brian responded before she could say another word. "How do you know if it's bull if you don't even know what he's talking about?"

Diana snapped back, "Do *you* know what he's talking about?"

"No, but it's worth my while to find out."

"Well, it's not worth a shit to me," she retorted as she stomped her foot on the ground.

"Okay, you just keep up that attitude and you're going to be real happy," Brian explained.

"What do you care? You don't even know me!" she snarled.

"Well, it would have been nice to get to know you," Brian said sheepishly.

She paused for a long moment. "Really?" she asked.

"Yes, it would have been nice to know you," he said in a low quiet voice. Diana walked away slowly then stopped in her tracks and turned her head in thought. We glared at her as a strong gust of wind wisped through her tattered hair and baggy clothes. The gust nearly blew her over as she struggled to maintain her balance.

"Well…maybe…maybe…I'll see what this crap is all about," Diana said. Brian smiled.

"What do we have to do?" I asked.

"I'm not sure. On each of these tickets is a truth and we must discover their meaning somehow," Brian looked at the manila envelope.

"See, I told you this is bullshit. Who has the time or energy to do this? I'll tell you the truth…nothing matters."

"How can you say that?" Brian jawed back. "We were born to live not born to die. There has to be something more to life."

"Oh, yeah? Like what? I can't make sense of it, and we'll never know so what's the use in trying?"

"I think this could be pretty interesting. You might even be surprised at what you find," I said to her.

"I seriously doubt that," she muttered, looking away again. Brian eyed her in disbelief.

13

"What have you experienced that is so awful? Why are you so bitter?"

"You wouldn't understand, Mr. Happy-Go-Lucky."

"Oh yeah, try me," he snapped.

"I don't want to get into it; let's just drop it." Diana became aloof as she stared at her hangnails once again.

"Okay, we can drop it for now, but if I'm going to be your experience partner, I'm sure these things will surface again."

"Whatever...don't count on it," she mumbled.

"Look, just because you're miserable don't try to pawn your unhappiness off on me, because it won't work," Brian exalted.

"I'm just being realistic, which is something you know nothing about, so just stick to your little fantasy dream world," she barked.

"I'd rather be living in a dream world, than a prison." I just stood silent, watching the positive and negative signs bounce off each other. I was a little embarrassed by their arguing but at the same time, amused. I was secretly chuckling to myself.

"Look, I knew this wouldn't work out, so just go with your other partner." Diana pointed at me rudely.

"Not so fast," Brian replied. "You're not getting out of this one. I'm not going to let you cop out on this."

"What are you going to do about it? Go tell the professor?"

"I'll tell you what I'm going to do, I'm going to...to...." He looked around, then at me, then back at her. "I'm going to take you to lunch. C'mon. Let's go." Diana's eyebrow raised in curiosity. Brian looked at me as I giggled.

The power of accurate observation is frequently called cynicism by those that don't have it.

—George Bernard Shaw

III

PERCEPTIONS AND MISCONCEPTIONS

We arrived at the overcrowded cafeteria and found ourselves in the midst of a meandering line of hungry students. It was like feeding time at the zoo. The banging of a million pots and pans rang in my ears as obnoxious students bumped into us. The lines could compare to Disney World.

"Great idea, rah-rah," Diana glared at Brian. "We're going to be here forever."

"It's really not a big deal, Diana," I said boldly. Her constant complaining was getting on my nerves. Like sardines in a small tin can we stood shoulder to shoulder, motionless as we held our lunch trays. Overly zealous students hastily rammed into to us while trying to order their food. Diana sighed in discontent as her body stiffened with impatience.

Eventually, we placed our lunch orders. Diana ordered a vegetarian plate, Brian a turkey sandwich, and I opted for a pasta dish with garlic bread.

"Excuse me, can you hand me a bottled water?" A tall, lanky man had tapped Brian on the shoulder.

"Sure." Brian grabbed one from the cold refrigerator stocked with rows of plastic bottles. "Is this one okay?"

"That's great, thanks," the man said.

"No problem," Brian replied. As we moseyed to the checkout, the gangly man stood behind Brian patiently. Diana's shoulders slumped as she let out a loud groan. Her lunch tray clumsily bumped into Brian's and the envelope from class fell off his tray, hitting the ground with a thud. The tall man beside Brian quickly bent down to pick it up off the floor.

"Here you go," he said, handing the envelope to Brian. "Are you in Dr. Jacobs' class?"   "Yeah, we just came from there. How did you know?"

"I could tell by the envelope. He's a colleague; we've done a lot of work together. So what do you think about his class?"

"It sounds really interesting, but we have no idea what he expects from us," Brian told him frankly.

"Don't worry—you will," he said laughingly.

"Is that a motto that all you philosophy professors use around campus?"

"Ha! No, not exactly. Actually, I'm not a professor; I'm a researcher. I study communication. I'm Dr. Nolan."

"Nice to meet you. I'm Brian and this is Diana and Madison. We're experience partners," Brian explained.

"Is it all right if I join you for a few minutes?" Dr. Nolan asked.

"Great," Brian said with enthusiasm. "We'll be sitting by the windows over there." He pointed in that direction.

With a warm smile the man said he would meet us in a few minutes.

"Who the hell was that?" Diana asked.

"He's a friend of Dr. Jacobs and wants to talk to us about the class."

"Oh great, he's exactly the person I want to have lunch with."

"Diana, this could be a good opportunity to get details about the class. Don't you want to know more about it?" I asked. Diana gave me a blank look and then rolled her eyes in disgust. Annoyed, I looked away.

"Diana, can you just lighten up? Does everything have to bother you?" Brian asked in exasperation. "He's just going to try to help us understand the class."

"Oh lucky me. Let's see what smarty-pants has to say," Diana said sarcastically.

16

Irritated, Brian looked at me as we both shared a sympathetic glance knowing exactly how the other was feeling. We found a table next to a bright window that overlooked the quad. Diana and Brian hungrily enjoyed their lunch as Dr. Nolan approached the table. He was confident and kind, with a self-assured, polite air about him. His small eyes and thick eyebrows gave him a distinguished look. His large ears stuck out from the side of his head slightly. I wouldn't call him attractive, but the way he carried himself was.

"Well, it's great meeting you guys. You're in for a very enlightening class." Dr. Nolan casually sat down next to Diana. "In fact, you're fortunate to have Dr. Jacobs as opposed to the other professors who teach the course. Jacobs brings a new philosophy to his teachings."

Diana interrupted him. "We don't get what he's talking about. It sounds like a bunch of crap, if you ask me."

"Well, a lot of students feel that way at first, but what you will experience will change your mind," he told us.

"What are we going to experience?" I questioned.

"Well, first let me explain to you the nature in which we experience things, or the way in which we gain knowledge about the world.

"How does that help?" Diana asked.

"Can you just listen please, Diana?" I begged.

Dr. Nolan continued. "You probably never realized this, but ever since we were children we have gained knowledge based on three basic principles: conformity, custom, and direct experience. First I'll touch on conformity.

"Throughout civilization, people acquired their beliefs about the world based on conformity or simply by agreeing with others. They found that agreeing with others about the world made it easier to coexist. For example, everyone in the Middle Ages agreed that the world was flat; therefore, believing in something that was universally thought of as true created a commonality between people. It also created a feeling of safety and security in knowing that everyone shared the same universal truth. Having all the answers already provided allowed individuals to establish a sense of comfort.

"Knowledge based on conformity is easy because everyone shares the same viewpoint. We all think that the earth is the only planet in the universe with civilization, right? This is because we have conformed to scientific views and universal views that say this is what we should believe. There is safety and security in knowing that everyone shares the same views about the world."

I thought about what Dr. Nolan had just said. "What about Roswell and UFO sightings?" I asked.

"That is correct, Madison, but by having that belief you are going against the conformity of the universal truth that there are no aliens. If you strongly believe that there are aliens in the universe there are thousands of scientists and government officials that would condemn you and undermine your opinion. Isn't that a scary thought?" he asked. "Isn't it frightening to know that many people would try to suppress your beliefs and ridicule you for believing them?"

I thought about it and nodded. "Yeah, I guess you're right."

"However, beliefs based on conformity pose problems because simply agreeing with the truths of the worldview forces you not to think for yourself and narrows your mentality. People merely go on believing something whether it's right or wrong. By simply agreeing or conforming to beliefs, we are limiting ourselves because it draws us away from discovering the real truth."

"But how does one go about finding the real truth? And doesn't it take up too much time and energy?" Diana blurted out.

"Yes, that's why it's so easy to believe something just because others believe it. You don't have to think about it; you just blindly believe it to be true because it's easy. You don't have to waste your energy. However, taking a different stand or viewpoint requires us to use some energy and actually think outside of the box. Most people don't like to do that."

"So you're saying that most people don't want to have their own beliefs because they are scared and lazy?" I asked.

"Yes, they don't want to put forth the effort of actually thinking something through because that could lead to frustration and cause confusion. In addition, it takes a lot more strength to put yourself on the line and stand alone against others. Most people would rather not know if what they believe is right or wrong because if it is wrong that will defy their logic. Also, people are scared to have their own beliefs because they might discover an answer that they don't want to know. But most importantly, they might discover something about themselves that they don't want to confront. That is why people find comfort when beliefs are shared with others." We thought about that for a moment as we ate our lunch.

"Have you ever questioned the beliefs of your parents?" Dr. Nolan asked us. "What do they always say? I don't want to talk about it. Right? Because somehow, avoiding the topic or situation is easier than actually confronting it. Have you ever heard the saying, ignorance is bliss?"

"But if you avoid these questions, how does one find happiness?" Brian wondered.

"You'll learn about that later. But let me finish my point. We also gain knowledge based on custom. These traditions are based on what prior generations believed. The beliefs came from traditional family believes that have been passed down. Can you think of a tradition that your family has?"

"Our family always opens our Christmas presents on Christmas Eve night just before midnight because that's how my parents celebrated Christmas when they were young. So opening presents on Christmas morning seems wrong to me," shared Brian.

"That's exactly right, Brian. What about you, Diana, can you think of traditions in your family?"

"Well, I can remember being about ten years old and I was over at a friend's house making macaroni and cheese. It was a tradition in my house to always have a certain kind of macaroni and cheese, and I realized that the brand my friend was preparing was not the brand my mom always bought and I refused to eat it. I automatically thought it had to be bad or something."

Dr. Nolan smiled brightly. "Yes, even though it was probably the exact same thing. But because there was a different label on the box, you thought it was wrong and bad. So your traditional beliefs made you think that since the macaroni and cheese wasn't the brand you were used to it had to be wrong and you refused to eat it. You didn't take into consideration that your belief based on tradition could be wrong. This is precisely what I'm trying to convey."

"Religion is a great example of beliefs based on tradition. We have religious beliefs that are derived from our parents, and their parents, and their grandparents' parents, and traced down through the family tree. For example, if your parents believe in Catholicism, chances are that you will also believe in it."

"But how do you know if it's the right religion?" I asked him.

"Well, if you believe in it, isn't it right?" Brian asked.

"If you can feel your religion's spirituality in the depths of your soul, then it's the right one for you. However, if you merely believe in a religion to appease your parents and you don't feel it penetrates your soul, or if you don't feel enlightened by its message, then you should question your beliefs and discover a new spirituality that is true to you."

"Being true to yourself is the most important aspect of life. If you deny yourself the truth, then you become out of balance, and that inconsistency will be detrimental to your life experiences.

"Your life experience encompasses everything—your attitude, your mind, your body, your spirit, and all of these things ultimately affect your health, and your personal well-being. If our life experiences are not in alignment with our own truth, then we become out of balance and out of sync with our true selves. This imbalance is also known as 'off the chosen path.'"

We all sat pondering for a minute while taking bites of lunch. The food didn't seem nearly as important to us. As I took a bite of my spaghetti, I felt a rush of sudden energy pulsating through my body as if I was more alive and more in tune with the moment.

"Let me get this straight," I proceeded. "If you lie to yourself about your experiences then that inconsistency will affect everything you do in life?"

"That's right, Madison. People become out of balance or out of touch with their purpose. Thus, not being true to yourself is a self-defeating process that snowballs into bad situations that are often very difficult to overcome. Hence, we have drug abuse, alcoholism, depression, and anxiety. These are addictions and bad habits that people develop when they are out of tune with their life purpose and life experiences. That is why recognizing our beliefs and why we have them is a very integral part of our well-being.

"Another way we learn about the world is by authority."

Diana interrupted, "I don't learn from authority figures."

"Please allow me to finish. "What do we do when we get sick?" he asked.

"We go to the doctor," Brian said.

"Right, because authority figures are specialized and efficient. It's easy to think 'I don't know what to do about this cold so I'll see an expert and he'll tell me how to fix it.' But what happens if this person is wrong? Don't you think that experts have their own biases based on their own beliefs?"

"Everybody has biases, right?" Brian inquired.

"For the most part, yes. To help you understand knowledge based on authority let me tell you an experience I had with an authority figure. The drain in my bathtub was backed up and it was causing a serious problem. I tried using various plumbing products from the hardware store but none of them worked. I don't know that much about plumbing so I called a plumber to fix it. He told me I needed to change a crucial pipe in order for the bathtub to work properly again. Without thinking twice, I told him to do whatever was necessary to get the job done right. He finished the job and charged me seven hundred dollars. After a week, a friend of mine came to visit that had the same service done on his own bathroom a few years back and told me that his service only cost a hundred and fifty dollars. Obviously, I had been duped by someone I considered to be an expert and professional in his field. So, it is apparent that authority figures are biased and often don't have your best interest at heart. In turn, there are many advantages and disadvantages about gaining knowledge through authority."

"So how does all this help us with class?" Diana asked.

> Truth #1—*Your human inquiry or the way you perceive the world is a vital part of your life experience and it shapes you into the person that you are.*

"This is truth number one."

"What do you mean by human inquiry?" I asked with interest.

"The way in which you perceive the world.

"Direct experience is another way that we gain knowledge about the world. The been-there-done-that philosophy. We believe firsthand experience and give it power."

"Okay, I touch a burning stove and learn that it's hot," Diana interjected.

"Right, but it goes much deeper than that. We pay very little attention to what is really going on around us and our observations are full of mistakes. Mistakes that we perceive to be true."

"I'm not sure I'm following you," Brian said.

"I'll give you an example how our direct experiences are often inaccurate and we give them power as if they are accurate. A couple weeks ago, a friend and I were eating dinner at a restaurant. I don't know how it started but we ended up having one of those conversations when you just can't stop laughing. We were laughing so hard our stomachs started hurting. No matter what we did, we could not stop laughing. Well, at the table next to us was a rather large, overweight woman eating dinner alone. She kept glaring over at us, clearly getting angry. We continued to laugh about whatever it was we were laughing about. Suddenly, she walked over to our table and asked, 'Do you have a problem with the way I look?' We tried to stop laughing. We looked at her and said, 'No.'

"Then she replied, 'I find it very rude that you're laughing at me because I'm overweight.' She walked out of the restaurant angrily. We were shocked to say the least. The experience that she took from the restaurant was that two rude men were laughing at her because she was overweight. So, every time she goes to that restaurant again, she will think of that experience—an experience that she holds as true but, in

PERCEPTIONS AND MISCONCEPTIONS

fact, is very wrong and inaccurate. Because she felt insecure, she immediately thought she was the cause of our laughter. She made an observation that fit her expectation and then made an error in her conclusion. She completely over-generalized her experience," Dr. Nolan proclaimed.

"We're all guilty of doing that," said Diana.

"That's correct. Everyone makes errors in reasoning. These errors develop into premature closure. That's when we make snap judgments and then stick to them because we think they are true. Think about it. Haven't you experienced a situation when, for one reason or another, you decided that you don't like someone very much? Every time you see that person, you're thinking you don't like him or her. Isn't it hard to break that pattern of thinking?

"We're all guilty of making quick judgments about something or someone and then sticking to that belief. Often after we make a judgment, we keep it to ourselves and then look for others to agree with us. This makes us feel better because when people agree with us it validates our perception of that person, and you tend to feel less guilty about your beliefs about someone else if your friend shares the same feelings about them. We always want to confide in a friend that agrees with us because we are always looking for a support system. However, if a friend disagrees with our opinion, it forces us to think that maybe our judgments were wrong and we all hate being wrong."

We listened attentively as Dr. Nolan spoke. I found this very interesting; I was so in tune with him and everything he said penetrated me.

He continued. "This leads us to the point that we often discount observations that don't fit our expectations. When we encounter situations that don't fit our beliefs or expectations, we think that encounter had to be wrong. We would rather classify the experience as a mere fluke than change our thinking patterns. Can you think of an example of this?"

"I think I can," Brian interjected. "You're at a party thrown by a fraternity house. Your expectation is that frat guys are shallow jerks. Then you start socializing with them and your impression changes. You start to believe that they're okay and decent after all. But when you ponder your experience the next day you rationalize the situation by thinking they were just being nice because they had a couple drinks, but they are still jerks."

"That's exactly right, Brian. Although you don't realize it, your snap judgments are very hard to break." Brian looked pleased with himself. "Another point I want to make is that we only recognize what we want to recognize. We actually see very little of what is really going on around us. And we notice only what we care to notice."

"What do you mean? I see things," Diana said.

"I'll give you an example of this. My friend Nancy had been married to her husband for five years. They had reached the point in their lives where they were ready to have children and start a family. They tried and tried to conceive for a year but were unsuccessful. Nancy was very upset and disappointed. She wanted very badly to have a child and that was all she could think about. It began to consume her every thought. Then the strangest thing started happening. She would walk down the street and see a pregnant woman. She would stand in the grocery line and she would be behind someone that was pregnant. She would sit down to have lunch and right next to her would be a pregnant woman eating. She would go to work and find out someone in the office was pregnant. She would turn on the television and find a pregnant woman in the commercial, and this went on and on. Everywhere she looked she noticed pregnant women."

"Oh that's just a coincidence," Diana said.

"There are no coincidences." He paused and looked at each of us. "If she hadn't been thinking about getting pregnant so much, would these same occurrences still have happened?"

"Yes, they would have," I replied. "But she just wouldn't have noticed them as much."

"That's right, Madison. We take in very little of what is happening around us. We only observe what is significant to us at the time and only see what we want to see. Our observations are full of mistakes. We must remember to notice what is around us and stop going through life only concerned about our own situations. Once you can do that, your life will open to new discoveries you never could have imagined. That is why we must eliminate making judgments, because judgments are biases that are constructed by our own insecurities and negativity."

"Insecurities?" Diana repeated.

"So what happened to your friend, did she ever get pregnant?" I asked.

"Yes, she did." Dr. Nolan smiled. "They now have three children.

"Well guys, I hope this discussion about human inquiry was helpful, and I hope you enjoy the class. Trust your intuition and go with the flow. I got to run." He gathered his belongings and started to move in his seat.

"Wait, wait, I have more questions," Brian exalted.

"I'm late for a meeting. Sorry, guys."

Dr. Nolan took his belongings and walked away, leaving all three of us with our thoughts reeling. We looked deeply at each other in wonderment.

"That makes a lot of sense," Brian said, looking straight at Diana.

"Well, I never really thought of any of this stuff before."

"I never realized how important our perceptions are and how they alter our experiences—either negatively or positively," I exclaimed. Brian looked away, pondering what just transpired, as Diana finished the rest of her lunch.

"Isn't it odd that we were at a moment of total confusion when we walked into the cafeteria and then we randomly bumped into Dr. Nolan?" Brian remarked.

"I was just thinking that," I said in amazement. "We found him at the most opportune time. Isn't that bizarre?"

I looked into the envelope from class and pulled out the first ticket. I could not believe what I saw. "Look at this," I said. Brian and Diana leaned in to see what was written on the ticket. It said, "Perceptions of human inquiry."

"That was exactly what Dr. Nolan discussed with us," Brian said with exhilaration. We looked at each other wide-eyed. Who was Dr.

Nolan, and how did we randomly find him at just the right moment? How do the other truths build upon our perceptions of human inquiry? I automatically felt a sense of brilliance—of mystique and intrigue. I felt light and empowered. I had a feeling of surreal clarity, and I could sense my energy rise. Everything seemed to be magnified as if I could see more vividly and in more detail. I could see Brian's and Diana's eyes sparkle as their faces glowed with a shimmer of iridescent magnificence. The light from the adjacent window poured through the glass as we beamed in wonderment.

*Whether you think that you can or that you can't,
you are usually right.*

—Henry Ford

IV

FORCES OF NATURE

The revolving door swung open as a rush of spring air blew through Brian's curly hair. We exited the cafeteria as Diana slowly shuffled her feet, but her step no longer seemed as methodical as before. We walked down the tree-lined sidewalks of the quadrangle and with every breath and every step we felt lighter and more alive. The birds sang playfully, enjoying the weather.

Hope springs eternal, I thought to myself as I walked with a slight bounce in my step. I observed the beautiful surroundings of the quad as students passed hurriedly to their respective destinations. I suddenly felt more appreciative of the beauty around me. As we walked, we took in the beauty of the flowers; the appreciation for them gave us a feeling of euphoria. Suddenly, there was a turning point in the sidewalk path.

"Well, what do we do now?" asked Diana.

"I'm not sure," Brian said.

"Are we just going to wander around all afternoon?" she asked sarcastically.

"Yeah, maybe that's what we should do, just to see what happens," I suggested.

"This is crazy, you know that?" Diana spat the words at me.

"I think this is what Dr. Jacobs and Dr. Nolan were trying to convey when they said to follow our synchronicity and go with the flow," I retorted.

"Are we looking for anything in particular?" Brian asked me.

"No, I don't think so," I responded with a smile. We continued to walk along the red and brown brick sidewalk, passing under large oak trees that draped over us protectively. The immense branches shielded us from the sun's glare as the leaves whistled in the wind.

"What does the next truth say?" Brian asked. "We need a clue, something that will help us know which way to go. We need to know what we have to discover next."

"I'm not sure if we should look in the envelope or just let the truths come to us," I said with skepticism.

"Just open the frickin' envelope," Diana snapped.

"Even if I open the envelope and read the next truth we won't know what it means unless someone explains it to us and helps us learn it," I told her.

"This is so stupid. I can't believe I went along with this," she responded disgustedly.

I could tell she didn't want to continue with us.

"Are you going to open the envelope?" Diana snarled

"I…I don't know," I said. "I don't think I should just yet."

She huffed at me and dragged her feet like a child. Brian just stared at her. She mumbled something under her breath. I didn't care what she said.

Off the quad, we arrived at a rounded brick circle. The shaded circle created a nook between the powerful academic buildings, portraying a peaceful retreat from the bustling sidewalks of the quad. The brownstone that outlined the circle was decorated with French gothic detail. Vivid flowers and green shrubbery created a tranquil ambiance. The circle was a popular gathering place where students read, studied, or created a personal private escape amidst their overwhelming studies. I perched myself on one of the marble benches, feeding off the beauty of the environment. My body felt light and uplifted, almost as if nothing could bother me. I felt rejuvenated. Content. Not even Diana's pessimism could bring me down.

"This is a beautiful circle. I never noticed it before," Brian proclaimed.

"Yeah, it's pretty cool," Diana said, understated.

"Isn't it funny how there are so many things we don't take the time to fully appreciate?" I asked. We sat down to rest for a minute and enjoy the breeze. There were a couple of people in the circle reading, writing, or just relaxing. I sat next to a scholarly-looking woman who was reading a book. She wore no makeup, but had a natural, homely appeal. Her hair lay straight and still on her bony shoulders. She had hazel brown eyes that looked calm and peaceful. As she read, tiny crow's feet crinkled around her eyes. She appeared to be in love with what she was reading. The book made her whole body smile.

Brian looked around and then glanced at Diana. "So what do you think about today so far?" Brian inquired.

"It's been all right, I guess." Diana said matter-of-factly.

"Just 'all right'? I think it's been great."

"You would."

"What's that supposed to mean?"

"Nothing." Diana looked away.

Brian looked at her inquisitively. "Here we go with your 'feel sorry for me' attitude again."

"What?" Diana snapped. "I don't want your pity."

"Oh, yeah? You don't, huh? Then why do you always make those kinds of remarks?"

"What remarks?" Diana asked, playing dumb.

"You know, those remarks that make me feel guilty or something. Like you're telling everyone 'feel sorry for me, my life sucks, everything sucks.'"

"What about you? You're always probing me with questions about what I think and how I feel. Can't you just let me be?"

"I'm just curious to see how you're experiencing everything."

"Well, when I feel like telling you, I will."

"What the hell did I say?" Brian asked sincerely.

"Figure it out!" Diana barked at him.

They sat in silence as Brian looked uncertain.

Again, I felt embarrassed in the middle of their squabbling. Being around an argument when you're not directly involved is not a fun spot to be in. It made me feel uncomfortable and awkward. I opted not to take sides. I sat there looking down at my Swiss Army watch, playing with its worn leather band. I wanted to tell Diana to lighten up. I swear I had never met a moodier person in my life. Someone should have put her in her place a long time ago. But then again, Brian was a little annoying with his eagerness to learn and his goody-goody persona. *But who am I to say anything, or think anything for that matter? I should take Dr. Nolan's advice and not judge. I don't really know their life story or anything.* But something told me I would know it eventually.

Suddenly, a rush of students burst through the doors of the buildings around the circle. I looked at Brian and Diana as the boisterous students settled around us, occupying the once peaceful space with loud academic conversation.

Flailing arms and dominant expressions radiated from the students' energetic bodies. They threw their book bags and notebooks about while communicating enthusiastically about what transpired in their classes ten minutes earlier. They all looked so alive, so full of life. And here I was sitting with two people who were constantly at each other's throats. Brian and Diana were suffocating in a cloud of gloomy despair.

With their shoulders shunned, eyes distant, they desperately held onto their own security for dear life. Then I heard the smiling woman next to me move in her seat. She appeared to be suddenly uncomfortable, trying to find a pleasing position but could not. She stopped reading, looked up, and turned her head toward us. "What could possibly be the problem with you two? It's such a beautiful day."

Brian and Diana were dumbstruck. They looked at her in shock. Since Diana and Brian's chins had dropped to the ground, I decided to answer. "They're just two polar opposites," I said with a sarcastic chuckle. "Don't mind them."

As soon I said that, the woman looked at me inquisitively. She paused, took her glasses off, and brushed the thin brown hair off her milky face. She stared directly at me.

"So they are like positive and negative forces?" she asked me.

"Yeah, I guess you can say that," I said, starting to wish I hadn't opened my mouth in the first place.

"Hmm…." She sat and thought for a minute. "That's interesting."

"What is so interesting about that?" Diana asked her.

"Have you ever heard of the forces of energy?" the woman asked.

We all looked at each other and responded, "No."

"Well, let me tell you about it." She continued. "There are three forces in the world: positive, negative, and neutral. The universe is a combination of all three forces of energy. In fact, every living, breathing organism or atom—no matter how small or how large—contains these forces.

"What about people?" Brian asked.

"People contain all three forces of energy as well. However, usually one force dominates."

"How do the forces get there?" I asked.

"They are created by each individual." We just looked at her.

"What?" I asked quietly.

"Yeah, that's right—they are created by each individual. A person creates his or her own force of energy and then tries to give it to others. This is more relevant with the positive and negative energy."

"How exactly are they created?" Diana asked.

"I'll get to that in a minute. First, do you have a few minutes to do an experiment?

"Sure," Brian said.

"I want you to close your eyes and relax. Clear your mind and try to think of nothing." We sat still for a few moments. It was a difficult task. I don't think there was a clear mind within fifty feet of us.

"Try to slow your thoughts down so that there is silence." I tried to clear my mind but it wasn't easy. Thoughts kept creeping in. "Peace," the scholarly woman said. "Relax," she said in a soothing calm voice. We tried to clear our minds for a few minutes with our eyes closed.

"Now that you have cleared your minds, I want you to focus on the word 'time.' Just think of 'time,'" she said. Our eyes were closed as we sat on the marble benches of the circle with the sun's light on our faces and the wind blowing through our clothes. I tried to focus. *Time, time, time,* I thought to myself. *Why time? What was significant about the word time?*

"Think about how this word makes you feel, what you associate with it, and what images it conjures up for you. How does it make your mind, body, and spirit feel? I want you to feel this word and let it penetrate and encompass your body." With eyes closed, I concentrated on "time" and I associated meaning to the word. I thought about what it meant to me and how it made me feel.

Clearly not wanting to take part in the experiment, Diana sat there breathing heavily out of her nose and panting from her mouth. She was barely even closing her eyes. I could feel the tension in her body. Eventually, our bodies slowly settled down and we were in concentration. But I could tell Diana was still a little tense. Brian, however, seemed to be enjoying this.

"Now that you are thinking about time, I want you to concentrate more deeply. Make this word embody you completely as if you become 'time' yourself." I wasn't quite sure what she meant by this. It sounded strange. *Let the "time" become me.* I just went with it. I concentrated and focused deeply. *I am time,* I thought, *and time is me.* I could feel myself getting more deeply involved in this concept. With every breath and every passing second I was becoming time and time was coming over me. My body grew heavy, and my breathing became more rhythmic as if I was in a deep trance. It felt different. Like nothing I had ever experienced. I was clearly awake and coherent to what was going on around me, but I was completely focused on the concept of time. I kept repeating the word "time" in my head. *Time, time, time.*

This went on for several minutes. I didn't think that we appeared silly or strange to other students in the area. And I really didn't care. All I thought about was time.

The woman tapped Brian on the shoulder. She said, "I want you to tell me what you're feeling and thinking."

FORCES OF NATURE

"Should I open my eyes?" he asked.

"You can if you want, or you can keep them closed if that helps."

He kept his eyes closed. "I feel that time is a very interesting concept."

"How so?" she asked. "Can you explain in more detail?"

"Time made me think of the future and I felt as if it were on my side. It made me happy to think that I have so much to look forward to and that there is so much I still want to do with my life and my time here. It made me feel energized and full of life. I was looking ahead and thinking of graduation and all the things I still want to accomplish."

"How did you feel overall?" she asked.

"Happy, I guess."

"So you associated happiness with the word 'time'?"

"I think I could explain it as more of a happy anticipation," Brian said, smiling. "I was thinking about my life and that made me happy."

"Very good. Is there anything else you felt?"

"No, I pretty much felt happy."

"Can I open my eyes now?" Diana blurted out impatiently.

"Yes, you may open your eyes," the woman answered calmly.

"How did *you* feel about this experiment?" she asked Diana.

"Couldn't you pick a better word than 'time'?" Diana asked. "It's so relative. Honestly, I thought this was a waste of 'time.'" Diana chuckled at her joke and looked at us to get a reaction.

Brian and I looked at her in silence. I couldn't believe she could be so rude and ungrateful.

"Is that really what you thought, Diana?" I asked.

"The word 'time' always makes me feel pressure. I don't like thinking about time and how we all know that the only certainty in this life is that one day we will die. That is the only thing that we know for sure. So I guess 'time' makes me think of how everything must end. That is why time is even measured because one day it will end. Right?" The woman nodded. I was shocked that Diana felt this way. It seemed so morbid, so miserable, so depressing.

33

The woman looked at Diana and asked, "You associate time with death?"

Diana looked at us and shrugged. "Yeah, I guess I do." We all sat silent for a moment. I didn't know what to think about this. I suppose many other people associate time with death, but that seemed very wrong to me.

"Well, Madison, what does 'time' mean to you?" Brian asked. I looked at him and paused for a second trying to collect my thoughts.

"Umm...." I was having trouble finding the right words. Sometimes, I found it hard to articulate what I truly felt from an experience. Some experiences are felt so deeply that it's difficult to make others comprehend exactly how I feel merely by communicating words, but I'd try to do my best to make them understand. I cleared my throat.

"Well, at first I started thinking about my life and the future and I felt excited. I thought about where I've been and how far I have come. I was also thinking about all of the great experiences that I have had and how every single one has shaped me into the person that I am right now. Especially the bad experiences—they jumped out as the most important because they really made me grow and taught me many lessons that I would have never learned if I had never experienced feelings of pain and sorrow. The bad experiences that I've had have made me change and grow as a person." The scholarly woman nodded her head a few times, took her glasses off the top of her head, and rested them on her pointy nose.

"Please, go on, Madison," she urged.

"When you advised us to think of time and make it embody us, I started feeling very different. At first, I didn't understand what you meant. So I just tried to clear my mind. I didn't have any expectations or preconceived ideas of how I was supposed to feel by this. I just went with it and tried to concentrate on opening up to this concept.

"For a minute, I didn't think anything; I was merely trying to concentrate on what you had said. Then the most amazing thing started to happen. I started paying attention to my breathing. Slowly, in and out, in and out—I was cognizant of it. I felt my lungs working to fill with air, and then letting go of the air into the world. It was like a deflating balloon. It seemed that each breath was going into the future because of every breath that I had taken before. I realized that if it wasn't for the previous breaths I had taken in my lifetime, I wouldn't have the next breath or even the next breath. The previous breaths were shaping my new breaths. Each breath was taking me into the future. Each new breath was carrying my mind, body, and soul into the unknown future.

"I began realizing that *I am time*. My entire being is time. Every second, every millisecond, there are incredible things going on in my body that are changing and progressing into the future. There are more skin cells forming, hair and nails growing, there are food and nutrients going through my bloodstream. There are brain signals transporting information faster than the speed of light, and there are thousands of new cells forming from the old ones.

"It's ironic because I know that all these things are occurring but I never took the 'time' to fully appreciate the beautiful processes that are going on inside of me and outside of me every second of my life."

The woman nodded and smiled. "This is very interesting, Madison. Please go on. What else did you feel?"

I cleared my throat again and tried to recall what else had come to mind during our experiment. "The best way I can put it is as the clock keeps ticking into the future, so do our body clocks. In fact, we work together. We are a tangible object that makes the intangible 'time' relevant. Therefore, I am time, and time is me. We are spiritual beings having human experiences. Up until this moment, I thought we are humans trying to have spiritual experiences. The truth is, we are all spiritual beings experiencing human knowledge based on everything we have learned from our previous moments. I had never thought of this before but somehow I felt this concept."

"What are you talking about, Madison?" Diana asked angrily. "Time is an intangible thing. How can we be like time?"

"You wouldn't understand, Diana."

"Maybe I can explain," the woman interrupted. "Let's analyze what just transpired. The word 'time' is neutral. It has no meaning unless one assigns meaning to it. So essentially the word itself is neutral and impartial unless someone assigns a value to it.

"When I asked Brian how he felt during the experiment about the word 'time' he said he experienced a sense of joy and happiness. He associated the word 'time' with the future and his excitement of things to come. The word filled his mind with his life, and the life occurrences that he still has to experience. Brian looked ahead into the future and was filled with pleasure and elation at the word 'time.' This is a very optimistic viewpoint. His mind associated feelings of happiness, and therefore his body felt the same way.

"Brian's feeling of joy is derived from his optimism. Optimism is positive. So Brian took a neutral situation—the experiment—and the neutral word 'time' and created a positive experience for himself. The feelings of happiness and joy are what Brian wanted to experience and so he did. The mind is very powerful. We all have the power to use our minds to create any experience that we want based on the way we work with our mind.

Truth #2—*You have the power over your mind. All encounters are neutral. You let them affect you positively or negatively. A clear mind will lead to unbelievable discoveries and revelations.*

"Wait a second," Diana said. "What do you mean 'work with our mind'? The mind does what it wants to do; I have no control over what I think."

"No, that's not true," the scholarly woman disagreed. "We choose because we have the power over our own mind. So if you know what's good for you, you can learn to make your mind your friend."

"Hey, that's pretty cool," Brian said with a chuckle. "I had no idea that I have the power to create my own experiences—either positive or negative. Everything, every situation, every thought, every idea is neutral. They only become positive or negative when we assign a positive or negative value or meaning to them."

I felt alive again, energized by this newfound discovery. I looked at my watch and noticed the minute hand ticking and I knew that no matter what, that minute hand would always keep ticking. I couldn't stop it like I tried to do early this morning. I was so foolish to get angry with that clock on the wall. Now I was perfectly content with what I had learned. I could tell my mind that time is all right with me. And it was.

"On the other hand," the scholarly woman went on, "Diana associated 'time' with unhappiness, despair, anxiety, and depression. She told her mind that the only measure of time is because we use it to validate that we will eventually die. She created a negative feeling about the experiment in her mind, and those thoughts developed into thoughts that are more negative and then more negative until it became death. Diana created that negativity all by herself. That was what she wanted to feel, therefore she did."

"Why is that?" I asked.

"It is because once you feel negative for a long time, those thoughts become a part of you and they encompass your entire being. It is very hard to break a negative thinking pattern because that cycle of thinking has been going on for so long, you actually condition yourself to think that way because that's what feels normal, or comfortable. The negative thinking takes its toll on everything you do. All those negative forces in your mind play havoc on your body and soul. They even cause health problems. Your own thinking creates the way you feel."

"So if you think bad thoughts, those thoughts create bad things to happen in your body?" Brian asked.

"Yes, that is correct. But if you think optimistically, good feelings will exist in your body, making you healthier than the negative thinker."

"I don't understand how this is scientifically possible," Diana stated.

"It is scientifically proven that each thought has its own energy wave. The positive thoughts have high energy waves and the negative thoughts have low energy waves. These high energy waves make you feel happy, content, and secure. The negative energy waves make you feel sad, moody, and depressed. Even words have their own energy wave. Using negative words, such as profanity, can bring you down as well. The negative brings you down—and those around you. That is why scientifically, energy forces are labeled with a plus sign for positive, and a minus sign for negative."

She continued. "I'd like to touch on the experience Madison had during our experiment. Madison had a neutral experience because she was clearly not feeling any negative thoughts for the word 'time'; however, she did have some positive thoughts about it. Later her thoughts changed to just being open-minded and not expecting anything negative or positive to occur. She concentrated on clearing her mind. She was merely open to absorbing her experience and going with the flow. This was relevant because she was so open, she actually began to think she was time and time became her. It is very important to realize that by not having any expectations, she was able to allow her mind to experience and discover new things.

"That is what being open-minded is all about. By being neutral with no positive or negative thoughts or expectations, we can experience, see, and feel things differently than we would before. To be open-minded is to absorb and let everything naturally flow into your thought process. However, this behavior comes from a lot of practice and experience at being open-minded. There are no preconceived notions or ideas either positive or negative. One just has to let it be. Once we can let it be, the mind is our very best friend and companion. Because you are your mind, you control your thoughts, and you can also control them to stop and gain clarity. By doing so, you can smell the roses, so to speak."

"What do you mean by that?" I asked.

"By just letting it be, you can accept energy without any positive or negative expectations," she explained. "By becoming neutral with no expectations, you become more connected to the energy source. Once you can accomplish this, you gain true clarity. When we are constantly struggling with our own mind instead of making it our friend, we become lost in a sea of constant misery because negative thoughts snowball into more negative thoughts. However, if we learn to slow down and try to gain a clear mind, we can gain inner peace and love. This is relevant in mediation in many Eastern religions. I teach Eastern religions and meditation here on campus. This is my area of expertise."

Ahh! Now it all makes sense, I thought, still listening to her wisdom.

"By conditioning the mind to be clear and open, new discoveries will be found," she went on to explain "These new discoveries and revelations will guide you into the right direction, thus enabling you to change and grow into the person you're meant to be. You will experience situations and events in a whole other light. This new light is particularly beautiful because it puts you in tune with who you are as a soul. It's also referred to as being connected to the source of energy. By conditioning your mind to become clear and open, you can discover your true self and your true calling. But you must become connected."

"Connected to what?" Diana asked.

The woman paused for a moment. "This source is the source of all living things. Religious people call this source God." Diana was listening attentively but said nothing.

"How do you discover your true self? Do the words just come to your mind miraculously?" Brian asked.

The scholarly woman pressed her lips together as if to speak, but then held back and looked at the ticking minute hand on her watch. She gathered her belongings.

"I really have to run to my next class," she said regretfully "I hope this was informative."

"But wait," I protested. "You didn't answer the question about how we discover our true selves."

"Be open, and don't let your ego and your insecurities get the best of you," she said. "You have to learn to let them go."

"What insecurities?" Diana asked apprehensively.

"How? How do you do that?" I asked.

"You'll figure it out," she said matter-of-factly. And with those words she vanished into the large academic building adjacent to us. All three of us were again left speechless. Diana grabbed the manila envelope and pulled out the next ticket. It read: "forces of nature." We were silent.

*The life that is unexamined
is not worth living.*

—Plato

V

MASK OF THE EGO

It was morning already and I was running late. The events of yesterday were so stimulating that I slept like a baby. I quickly got out of bed, threw some clothes on, washed my face, brushed my teeth, grabbed a granola bar, and started running. I looked like hell. I quickly snatched the powder compact out of my purse and applied some makeup to my face, then ran as fast as I could. I needed some lipstick to add some color to me. I normally never go anywhere without makeup. I felt naked without it. That's an insecurity of mine.

Class was close by, but I still needed to jog to get there on time. I had a real jerk of a professor who wouldn't let anyone in the class if they were more that two minutes late. He even locked the doors and counted students absent. More than two absences would lower my grade. I thought that was very rude of him, but if you're passionate about something, time is of the essence and accountability is key. Journalism was my passion, but I didn't know why.

My heart was doing somersaults in my chest as I ran up the stairs instead of taking the crowded elevator to the third floor. I skipped every other step with long strides. After class I was supposed to meet Diana and Brian near our little circle again. While running, I was thinking about what we'd experience today.

I was relieved when class was finally over. I arrived at the circle and noticed Brian and Diana sitting where I last saw them. I saw Brian sitting with his arms crossed over his chest, and Diana had her head down reading a book. I shouted their names.

"Hey, guys," I greeted. Brian smiled at me as Diana raised her head slightly. I was holding the manila envelope from class under my arm. Diana glared at the envelope. Brian's smile slowly dissipated. It felt strange knowing what we had experienced together yesterday. Seeing them today felt awkward. It was like having a one-night stand with someone and then bumping into to that person two days later.

Although we knew each other intimately, we were still strangers. We sat in silence, unsure of what to say or think. I began messing with my hair and playing with my necklace. Then I heard the most annoying noise. It sounded like the bottom of someone's pants was scraping against the concrete. I turned to see where it was coming from among the nuances of the densely populated circle and realized the source of the racket. I turned my head to notice a large bag overflowing with papers and books as it hung around a man's beefy, broad shoulders. He was short, round, and bald. The hair he still had on his head was taken from one side and combed over to the other side. His unkempt attire might classify him as simple, but his eyes said something else. They projected intelligence and kindness. His eyes laughed as we looked at him. He reminded me of a scholarly George Costanza from *Seinfeld.* His understated appearance was secondary to his amused face. He smiled to himself as he sat down next to me on the marble bench. He whistled while he opened a book and reached for a pen from his shirt pocket. His darting eyes skimmed from left to right across the pages. He read with delight and enjoyment as his eyes danced with the text. The wind blew quickly and I smelled a hint of garlic on his breath. He turned his head.

"It's a nice day, isn't it?" he commented, looking directly at me.

"Yes, it is," I remarked. He stared, gave me a puzzled look, and rested his pen onto his thin upper lip.

"Did you take my psychology class last year?" he asked.

"No, I don't think so."

"You remind me of another student; she was quite a character."

"Really? How so?" I wondered.

"Well, it's a funny story."

"I'm Madison," I said.

Brian overheard the conversation and immediately interjected. "I'm Brian, and this is Diana."

"Nice to meet you. I'm Dr. Pearson. I teach psychology."

"Are you two a couple?" Dr. Pearson asked, as he pointed at Brian and Diana with his pen. They both glared at each other and immediately blurted out a response.

"No."

"I can sense hostility in your voices."

"We're experience partners for a project we're working on," Brian explained. "I guess we're just a little frustrated right now." The man was assessing them as if Brian and Diana were his patients.

"Frustration is a state of emotion that is caused by many factors," Dr. Pearson said.

"What do you mean exactly?" I asked.

"Well, in order to understand the way we interpret emotions, you must find out about your own personality, and what your personality says about you."

"How are we supposed to do that?" Diana asked petulantly.

"It's important to recognize that personalities develop at a very young age and they derive from our desire for attention from our parents."

"So how does understanding our own personality help us understand our emotions?" Brian asked.

"Ever since we were children, we have all developed an ego trait, or way of gaining attention from others."

"Ego trait?" I repeated with curiosity.

"What I mean by ego trait is also called an insecurity. We use our insecurities on people to try to feel better about ourselves. How many times have you felt bad about a situation that was going on in your life and you used your insecurity on someone making the other person feel bad, so that you could feel better?"

"I don't think people intentionally want others to feel bad. They do it without realizing it," Brian proclaimed.

"See, people either have one dominant ego trait or sometimes they can use a number of them to reach their desired state of well-being," the round professor explained. "However, most people fall into one of four categories. The ego traits are: threatener, scrutinizer, indifferent, or sympathy traits. These traits range from aggressive to passive in nature. The threatener is the most aggressive trait and the sympathy trait is the most passive."

"Are these traits something that develop over time, or are we born with them?" I asked. The professor looked pleased at the question.

"They are developed during the first few years of life. We all have our own way of gaining attention from others. Attention is also classified as energy. When we are young, we look to gain energy from our parents. We are too young at that point to understand that we must gain energy from the source, so we look to our parents to compensate for that energy. We learn to manipulate a situation to achieve the feeling of well-being that we were accustomed to before we came into the world."

"What feeling?" Brian asked.

"We all have an internal state of being that is comfortable for us; however, everyone's comfort zone is different. What is comfortable for you, Brian, may not be comfortable for Madison or Diana, or vice versa. When that comfort zone no longer feels comfortable, or when we no longer feel good, we all strive to get back to our comfort zone, which is filled with the energy that we need. Some people require more energy or attention, and others don't need as much. But we will stop at nothing to achieve that internal comfort zone that we are familiar with. If our energy is low, we will not feel comfortable or happy. We become irritated, crabby, angry, and sometimes downright mean. So in order to get back to our comfort zone, we need more energy. We gain energy from food, sleep, our surroundings, and from other people.

"So what you're saying is that we are constantly struggling for energy?" I asked.

"Yes, Madison. We are always trying to gain energy so that we may feel good. The more energy we have, the better we feel. Ever since childhood we have all developed a way to manipulate things to acquire more energy. This manipulation developed into an ego trait. There are four different categories that people fall into.

"First, the threatener is someone you feel physically threatens you. This person uses this trait to gain energy by physically threatening or intimidating you to feel scared. That is how he or she gains energy from others. This person developed this trait because his parents or the most significant role models in his life threatened him as a child and the only way he felt comfortable in stressful situations was to threaten the other person back. Because the significant people in his life were threateners, and were stealing his energy by threatening him, the child learned that if he threatened back he would retrieve the energy that he lost."

"Are threateners only men? Or can woman be threateners too?" Brian wondered.

"Gender does not play a role in ego traits. A man or woman can develop any one of these traits, so yes, a woman can definitely be a threatener as a man can definitely have a sympathy trait."

He continued. "The next is the scrutinizer. This person gains energy by probing you for information. Once the information is received, he or she then scrutinizes your answers or responses. The reason they feel the need to do this is because of their parents' lack of attention or energy. Their parents were either working a lot or had other obligations and the child always felt lonely. Therefore, they were always left to ask where were you, Mom and Dad? Where are you going? When are you coming home? And so forth."

This struck a cord in me. I immediately thought of an old friend. "I can remember I had a friend who was a scrutinizer in high school. She would always probe me for personal information and then when I would tell her the news she would scrutinize and criticize my decisions and choices. She would always say stuff like, 'Gross! You think John is cute?' or 'Why do you want to go to that college? It sucks.' or 'Why are you wearing that? It accentuates your hips.' I finally got so upset with it, I called her out on what she was doing. I told her that I was tired of her constant criticism and that if she didn't have anything nice to say I didn't want to hear it. That really made her mad because she had no idea how she was acting. It wasn't like I needed her approval, but she always made me feel bad about myself, and eventually I decided I no longer needed her as a friend."

"Thanks for that example, Madison." The professor looked at me and smiled. "We need people who positively uplift us in a way that is beneficial, not detrimental. Energy is the key to your life. We gain energy from other people by the attention that they give us. That is why people that are around a lot of positive people can't stand to be around people that are negative because that negativity physically drains their energy. We all know how we feel internally and externally and we know how it feels to feel your own arm, your own leg, and your own head.

"We also know how we feel from the inside out. The internal feelings we possess are projected outwardly. This is conveyed by the way we walk, the way we talk, and the way we carry our bodies. However, most importantly, the way we think determines the way we feel. The way we think is a crucial element to your energy. The way we talk to ourselves internally dictates our personal well-being. Even the words we use trigger positive or negative thoughts. They even have their own energy levels. It's amazing how the words we use and the thoughts we have effect our energy either positively or negatively. The way we talk to our inner spirit every day is a vital part of discovering our true selves."

We listened closely to Dr. Pearson. He was actually reiterating what the scholarly woman told us yesterday. I was very interested about learning more about these ego traits.

"You see, kids, there are energy fields around each person. Depending on our energy levels and the way we feel, we can actually take from other people's energy. Or give energy to others."

"Can you give us an example of this, Dr. Pearson?" Brian asked.

"Have you ever been around someone who makes you feel good, makes you feel alive and happy? And you love to be around that person? That person makes you feel safe and secure?"

"Yeah, sure," we all replied.

"Well, that person was actually giving you energy from their own energy source."

"Did that person actually know they were giving you energy?" I asked.

"Probably not," Dr. Pearson replied. "If you don't know about it, it doesn't matter in your life. But once you are aware of energy fields and how they affect our daily lives, you will be more prone to recognize them."

"So how do we gain more energy? Brian asked.

"It's easy. You just have to stop what you're doing, take in your surroundings, and feel love deep within your being."

"Feel *love?*" Diana said. She spoke of it as if she had no concept of that four-letter word.

"Oh, no. *Love?* What is that, Diana?" I asked half-mocking her. Brian and I looked at each other and laughed aloud. Diana sarcastically stuck her middle finger in the air in our direction and turned her head. We continued to laugh even louder and harder than before. Dr. Pearson was examining us under his psychological microscope.

"You see what just happened there? Diana asked a legitimate question, then Madison scrutinized her question as Brian chimed in to help Madison. You both stole Diana's energy and in retaliation to try to get it back, Diana flipped you off. You see how this works? These kinds of interactions happen all the time, many times a day. Now, you realize that we are all trying to gain energy."

"What about the indifferent person? What are they all about?" I asked.

"The indifferent person gains energy by being secretive and mysterious. They never give out too much information so they keep the other person guessing or wondering what is going on. This makes the other person have to ask a lot of questions to try to get to the bottom of things," Dr. Pearson proclaimed.

"Why would someone want to be secretive? Don't you think communication is better when the lines are open and clear?" Brian asked.

"Sure, it's better to communicate openly but the indifferent person wants to hide their feelings, or be mysterious because somewhere in the past they have been scrutinized. Somewhere along the way their parents were constantly ridiculing them of their decisions or their actions. The scrutinizer, being their mother or father, was always probing them for answers and when the indifferent person would respond, the scrutinizer would always criticize their answers or undermine them. See, the scrutinizer steals energy from the indifferent by always asking questions and then criticizing all the answers. This forces the indifferent person to become more secretive and more mysterious because by withholding information the indifferent person can hold on and maintain their energy without giving any to the scrutinizer. By withholding information, the indifferent person actually gains energy from people because they force others to give up their energy by making them wonder what is going on with the indifferent person. The indifferent person leaves the scrutinizer to be left to answer their own questions."

"Oh, I see how it works," I said. "So the scrutinizers develop their children to be indifferent or aloof. But then what do threateners create?"

"That's a great question, Madison. That's actually my next point. Threateners create the sympathy trait," Dr. Person said.

"What's the sympathy trait?" Diana asked.

"The sympathy trait is created to gain energy from others by constantly wanting sympathy or pity from others. This person always makes you feel bad for them and draws you into a world that is filled with their personal despair. This person tends to complain a lot about situations and people. They also want others to feel sorry for them, as if their life has been so horrible. These are people that tell you their life story that is always filled with anguish and pain. They are always looking for sympathy and someone to listen to their worries and problems. They often dump their worries on anyone who will listen. Another characteristic of the sympathy trait is always blaming others for their own downfalls. Because somehow, to the person with the sympathy trait it's never their fault; it's always because of someone else or some other circumstance."

"How did they develop this sympathy trait from a threatener?" Brian wondered.

"Because the sympathy person always felt threatened by the threatener. Maybe their parents physically threatened them or verbally threatened them. Thus, making the sympathy person feel sorry for themselves. The sympathy person would try to make others feel sorry for them as well, to gain more energy. The goal of the sympathy ego is to gain energy from the threatener by guilt-tripping the threatener for making them feel so bad. As if to say to the threatener, look what you have done to me, look what you've made me become. Sympathy egos gain energy by making people feel pity for them."

"Does that sound familiar, Diana?" Dr. Pearson asked.

"I...I...I don't know...this is all new to me."

"So let me get this straight," Brian proceeded. "The threatener trait creates a sympathy trait, the scrutinizer creates an indifferent trait. But what trait creates the scrutinizer?"

"You guys are getting ahead of me," Dr. Person said, chuckling. "The indifferent ego creates the scrutinizer."

"How?" I asked.

"Because, Madison, by being aloof or mysterious it forces others to constantly ask questions. Let's say that you have the indifferent ego and you get married and have children. And let's say hypothetically that you had a real important career and are rarely home for your children. This would force your children to constantly ask you questions. 'Where are you, Mommy?' 'When are you coming home?' 'What's for dinner?' And so on. Then, when you would give an answer, they automatically wouldn't like it or approve of your answer. They might throw a tantrum or cry or have loud outbursts in an attempt to gain energy from you because your indifference or lack of attention was stealing their energy. So your lack of attention would make them feel bad, so they would have to make you feel bad. Does that make sense?" Dr. Pearson asked as he looked at all three of us.

He continued. "So because of the lack of attention from the indifferent trait the children become scrutinizers. And then scrutinizers' children become indifferent."

"Wow, this is really cool," I said. I glanced over at Diana as she looked at Dr. Pearson.

"There's one last trait you didn't cover," Diana said. "How does one become a threatener?"

"Because the threatener is the most aggressive of all ego traits, the threatener creates either one of two traits. The threatener creates either a sympathy trait, or another threatener trait. So, if someone is threatened as a child they may also become a threatener as an adult. You know the old saying either one becomes exactly like their parent or desperately tries to become the exact opposite. Well, that is the case with the threatener. The threatener will either create an equally aggressive ego trait or create the exact opposite or most passive trait, being the sympathy trait."

We all looked at Dr. Pearson with amazement. I sat there with my mouth open, wondering which ego trait I had and how was it was created. Then, I briefly thought about my parents and what traits they might have and how mine was created because of theirs. I found all of this information to be very enlightening. I realized that everyone has insecurities—that's just part of being human. I also knew that as human beings, we always try to protect or shield our true selves from others to avoid getting hurt, but I had no idea that everyone created an ego trait without knowing or realizing that they did it. *Come to think of it, I think I have realized that I do have an ego trait that I use on people.* I sat there still gazing at Dr. Pearson in amazement. Diana and Brian looked just as astonished as I was by this newfound wisdom.

"What you need to know is that everyone has an ego trait. Everyone is either a threatener, a scrutinizer, an indifferent, or a sympathizer."

Truth #3—One must drop their ego trait to get closer to who they really are. Because these ego traits take us further from the truth and less connected to the source. If you stay connected to the source you will have all the energy you ever need and you won't have to struggle to steal it from others.

FIRST CLASS TICKET

Dr. Pearson was right. I thought about all the energy struggles that I have had because of my lack of connection to what was really important.

"So, kids, this will give you something to think about. What ego trait do you possess? And how was it created?"

Dr. Pearson brushed his hand through his comb-over and gathered his messy book bag and stood up slowly. He looked straight at Brian and Diana as if he had something very meaningful to say.

"Just remember, if we let go of our ego traits we will become happier, more grounded, and more content. We won't have to keep fighting each other for energy or attention. By letting go of our ego traits we can gain true energy, happiness, and peace, and pass it on to others. Remember that. If you're not connected to the one true source of energy you are lost.

"Well, kids, it's been a pleasure but I must prepare for my next class. Good luck."

And with those last words he was gone. We sat there quietly. After a few minutes, Diana became restless with thinking as the lines on her forehead crinkled and the fire in her eyes burned.

"Hey, he didn't tell us how to get rid of our ego trait! This kind of thing always happens to me." She looked at each of us to agree with her complaining.

"So what do we do now?" Brian asked.

"Hurry up and wait," I said ironically.

Once you eliminate the impossible, whatever remains,
no matter how improbable, must be the truth.

—Sherlock Holmes *(by Sir Arthur Conan Doyle)*

VI

MISUNDERSTOOD TRUTH

The light was streaming in from between the vertical blinds as thin bright lines of sunlight made stripes on my face. I opened my eyes to a new day and I felt different. I hadn't really *changed,*, but I knew I wasn't quite the same. The philosophy class was making me feel like a kid in a candy store of wisdom.

I thought about Dr. Jacobs, Dr. Nolan, the scholarly woman, Dr. Pearson, and myself. I reflected on Brian and Diana, and why these two particular individuals turned out to be my experience partners. *What did I have to learn from them?* It all seemed very surreal. I laid sprawled out on my back staring up at the ceiling fan for a few moments, my thoughts jumping from one topic to another.

While lying on my back, hands behind my head, I stared at the ceiling fan spinning swiftly in full circles. The fan made a perfect three-sixty. Spinning around and around the fan moved constantly, never breaking stride, never faltering, never hesitating. *It spins, as the earth spins on its axis.* And then I thought, we too spin around and around. Every minute, every hour, every day, we spin miraculously. However, some of us fear the spinning, and others welcome it. Some don't even notice it, while others notice the spinning but do nothing about it. Some alter their perception of the spinning by wrong judgments, some protect themselves from spinning by creating ego traits, and some never even recognize they are spinning until they spin out of control.

I wasn't sure which category I fell into. I knew and recognized that I was spinning. And it was all that spinning that was making me well

51

rounded. Then my thoughts moved to the Plague and the baseball game she had invited me to. *I should call her and tell her that I'll go. It seems only right. I'll call her before my class,* I thought. *Then I'll run over and meet Brian and Diana for lunch.*

I took a shower, got ready, had my coffee, and was all set to call Rachel. I dialed her number and waited patiently. The phone rang and rang then suddenly her voicemail picked up. I left her a message to call me back. Then I remembered that I should call my mom. I hadn't spoken to her yesterday and she gets upset when I don't talk to her every day. She was a little overbearing and she worried a lot about my choices, but I knew it was only because she cared about me. *It would suck if no one cared about me,* I thought, so I didn't mind talking to her and keeping her abreast of what was going on in my life. I would listen to her ramble on about her dinner parties and her interior decorating ideas. I knew that was the stuff she enjoyed, and she was actually making me start to appreciate it.

My beat writing class lasted an hour and a half, and I walked out of class feeling completely alive. I was so energized by the professor's passion for writing and his profound knowledge on the subject matter. The assignment was to write a beat about a significant character we personally knew. Considering that I had met so many new characters in the past few days, I wasn't sure who I would choose. I knew that my direction was clear and that pursuing journalism was my personal calling as if I was laying out the blueprints of my future. Thinking about things to come always made me feel excited deep in the pit of stomach. Like the feeling you get when you're going down the big drop on a roller coaster. It was going to be a long journey and I knew it would be full of many bumps and unexpected twists and turns, but those bumps and bruises would make me a great journalist.

I thought about our conversation with Dr. Pearson yesterday, and my ego trait. My thoughts reverted back to our conversation with him. I wondered about how I acquired it as a child and what it said about me. My ego trait was aloof or indifferent. My parents were both scrutinizers. Apart from my mom's arts and crafts and dinner parties, I was her main focus in life. She was always disapproving of the choices I made. She would constantly probe me with questions and then dump on my answers. She would ask twenty questions and then find something wrong with everything I said. I knew it was because she cared. She didn't want me to get hurt.

But in my efforts to avoid being ridiculed for what I was about or what my plans were, I became indifferent and mysterious. By being mysterious I could gain energy from her because that would force her to constantly wonder about me, but never fully know the truth. That was how I gained energy. When my parents asked me questions, I would be as vague as possible so that I could make them think about why I was being mysterious, secretive, and vague. I would hold back information and let them guess about what was going on with me. Now that I thought about it, my ego trait was really holding me back from being the person I wanted to be. I can't use this tactic if I want to be a good journalist. I'll have to become an interviewer. I have to be the one asking the questions. I can't be aloof in that field of work.

I walked through the crowded quadrangle and stopped to say hello to some people I knew. I figured I had to do the petty small-talk thing. It's all part of the game. It's rare that I find anything these people say remotely interesting or entertaining but I make an appearance, and grin and nod and muse at what they have to contribute. I add my two cents to the conversation as well, though it usually feels forced and trivial.

But something was different today. I found that I was not playing the game. I was genuinely interested and intrigued by people, and by socializing with them I found that I was giving them energy and uplifting their spirit and they were doing the same for me. By looking into their eyes and smiling genuinely, I could feel their energy levels grow as I could feel my own growing. I didn't have to fake it or overdramatize anything. I was just being myself. Being genuine actually felt good. I'm always genuine to the people in my life that I love, but in some social circles I find that I hold back a lot about myself and never give out too much information. It's because of my darn ego.

I walked down the stairs of Tifton Academic Center with a smile on my face. I reflected on my interactions with others before and I noticed that even though I thought other people were being fake or vacant, I in fact, was the one who was being vacant, because I was holding back my true self. *Why was I doing that?* I wondered. That silly insecurity I developed from childhood was hindering my progress. Maybe if my parents hadn't constantly scrutinized me as a child, I wouldn't have this ego holding me back. But Dr. Pearson stated that I probably would have adopted another ego. If my parents were threateners, I would have developed a threatener or sympathy trait. And if they were indifferent, I would have been a scrutinizer. If my parents had sympathy traits, I would also develop a sympathy trait. Instead, I possessed an ego that does not let anyone in because I am afraid people will ridicule what I have to say.

If I want to be a journalist, I certainly can't be afraid of scrutiny because I will be dealing with it on a daily basis. There will always be an editor who will dump all over my work and make me change it. But I must stand firm of my convictions and not be afraid to speak my mind. I will always be scrutinized but I will learn how to deal with it.

Then it occurred to me that I was doing exactly what I needed to be doing. I had chosen a journalism career as a way of breaking my ego trait. I had chosen to break my ego trait indirectly, as if I had known it was there all along but now I actually knew how to label it. I had the indifferent trait. The more I thought about this on my way to the cafeteria, the more I realized how foolish I had been acting. *What a bunch of bullshit.* I felt like such a coward. So what if people don't like my ideas or what I had to contribute? They could scrutinize them all they wanted—I didn't care. The only person who mattered was me, and how I viewed myself. If others wanted to be fake, that was their problem, but I was not going to succumb to my ego anymore. I thought about what Dr. Pearson had said, how letting go of your ego will allow you to become the real you. It was stupid to have aloofness and I hated feeling like I was holding myself back from being myself.

I felt different—like I was changing for the better. But I knew that change is hard, and it takes a long time to break behavior patterns. I recognized that it would be a long process, but I felt it was a start.

My book bag swung over my shoulder as I walked briskly to the cafeteria to meet Brian and Diana. I was actually a bit nervous. I thought about how different they would seem to me today. It's always different after you spend a lot of time with new people. When you spend an entire day with someone and learn about them and experience new things together, it seems like you've taken three months of getting to know each other and compiled it into twenty-four hours. I wondered what new things would transpire today and how this would help us in our quest for discovering the other six truths.

I walked into the noisy, overcrowded cafeteria; again, it was a madhouse. I looked around for Brian and Diana but I didn't see them anywhere. We were supposed to meet at one-thirty near the pool tables. I looked at my watch and this time I wasn't late. I was actually right on time. I looked around a little more and then it happened. I stopped in my tracks and my mouth dropped to my ankles. There he was. The most attractive man I had ever laid eyes on was standing up against the wall reading a book. I was instantly drawn to him. I felt like I knew him somehow even though we'd never met. He stood out to me, as if a large yellow flag was draped over his body saying, *Notice me.*

I knew I should say something to him. But what would I say? Should I come up with some sort of cheesy line? *Have I met you before? Do I know you from somewhere?* No, I couldn't say anything like that. That would sound silly. Instead, I casually sat down at a table and pretended to read the college paper. I glanced up from the story every so often just to bat an eye.

He had a full head of dark curly hair, a well-defined jawline, full lips, and the most amazing green eyes. I was amazed by his rosy cheeks and red lips. He was so breathtaking he was almost pretty. His body was long and strong with broad shoulders and a thin waistline. His hands were manly with a hint of hair trickling down from his arm.

As I looked up from my faux paper reading, I noticed Brian walking in my direction so I decided to wait until he saw me even though I saw him first. He looked happy and refreshed as he glided across the room. *Where is he going? Doesn't he see me?* He kept walking past me. I said nothing—that damn aloofness. I knew I had to get past that somehow. I needed to break the ties that bound me. I had to do it. I wasn't going to continue to be a spectator in my own life and just watch things unfold before me without taking action. I could either sit it out or I could dance. I needed to dance. I needed to seize the moment. *Forget the aloofness,* I told myself. *It's only holding me back from my truth.* I fully recognized this now.

This is my chance to make all of the occurrences that have happened in the last two days come together. Brian's strides got longer as a large smile illuminated his face. *Where is he going? Is he walking over to...no, he couldn't be! I don't believe it. He's walking over to my man. How does he know him? Are they friends? This is too weird.* Brian approached him casually.

"What's up, dude?" I heard Brian ask.

"Hey, what's goin' on?" the beautiful man said. My heart was racing in my chest. *Should I walk over and introduce myself to him?* I sat there paralyzed. All I could do was stare as they continued to chat.

Then, a short and stocky blond guy I had never seen before walked up to them and started talking in a loud obnoxious voice. The blond guy was making stupid gestures and trying to crack jokes. He was bouncing all over the place. He was one of those guys you'd like to crack upside the head and tell him to shut up or turn it off.

No, get away, annoying boy; you're blocking my view. I glared at them completely enamored with this beautiful man. I couldn't believe Brian knew him. He and Brian continued to talk, sharing a few laughs. Then suddenly in the midst of their conversation Brian turned his head as if he felt my energy drawing into them. He gazed right at me. *Oh shit, Oh shit. No, he didn't just look at me. Oh my God, I am so embarrassed.*

"Hey, Madison." Brian walked over to me and gave me a hug. "I thought that was you," he said.

"Hi, Brian, how are you?" I returned the hug shyly, not wanting to appear too interested in him. I didn't want "the man" to think we had something going.

"Madison, I want to introduce you to my buddy." My stomach was in knots, I couldn't speak. I looked at "the man" standing over near the wall talking. I was drawn to him.

"No, please allow me to introduce myself." Brian gave me a blank look. I gathered myself, took a deep breath, and walked over to this beautiful, intriguing person.

"Hi, I'm Madison." I spoke with confidence and assurance as if I owned the situation. His eyes looked right through me.

"Hi, I'm Jeff.

"Hi, Jeff," I said with a wide smile.

"Jeff Greenberg," he stated looking at me as if I should recognize him. And with those words there was dead silence. I stared at him wide-eyed, my mouth hanging open. *This is Jeff Greenberg?* I thought. *No! This strikingly beautiful man that I feel a timeless connection to is Jeff Greenberg? No, this can't be happening. Why me? Why now? Why couldn't he be someone else? Why does he have to be dating the Plague?*

My head started spinning; I suddenly felt dizzy.

"It's nice to meet you," he said in a low voice. I shook his hand and felt a shock through my body. By taking his hand it immediately felt comfortable—familiar and real. It was as comforting and welcoming as coming home. It felt like I was home. We stood looking into each other's eyes for a long moment. I was still holding his hand. There were no words needed. I said nothing. All I could do was gaze at him in amazement.

I could see Brian staring at me out of the corner of my eye. I suddenly snapped out of it and said, "Nice to meet you too."

"What the hell, Brian?" the short obnoxious guy interjected. "Aren't you going to introduce me to your friend?"

"Troy, this is Madison," Brian said quickly, giving the short guy an irritated look.

The short blond guy gave me a wink and said, "How you doin'? I'm Troy Gunnison. I play shortstop on the baseball team. They call me the shortstop extraordinaire." He was trying to be cool. I was not impressed. I wasn't going to allow this guy to break my eagerness to communicate more with Jeff. I knew I needed to convey to him that I knew his girlfriend and that I was going to his baseball game.

"You should come see a game," he said, as he inched closer to me, smiling. Brian sensed that I was getting irritated by Troy, so he did his best to break it up.

"Have you seen Diana?" Brian asked.

"No, not yet," I said, turning back to look at Jeff.

"Let's wait for her by the pool tables," Brian suggested.

I decided to make a bold move. I gazed directly at him. I mustered up all my gusto. Then I asked, "Are you the same Jeff Greenberg who is dating Rachel Gibson?"

He looked at me surprised as if I caught him off guard. Then he smiled.

"Do you know her?" he asked.

I nodded, as Brian and I walked away from him. My heart sank to the pit of my stomach. I was so disappointed.

Why did he have to be dating her? What could he possibly see in her? I just didn't get it. But I was beginning to understand why I ran into Rachel the previous day. First that coincidence and now this. It was beginning to make sense. But what am I supposed to do about it? As I walked, I was floating on air. Wow, he was magnificent. But why does he have to be Jeff Greenberg of all people at this school? I had so many mixed emotions.

I walked with Brian over to the pool tables and saw Diana waiting there, her long black hair draping over her pale face. Her heavy book bag looked like it would cause her skinny body to topple over at any moment.

But Diana looked different. She appeared gentler, almost childlike in a vulnerable way. We walked closer to her and no longer had to kick down the colossal wall. Maybe the turmoil inside of her was subsiding.

Maybe the cold war was over and she was finally ready to crumble her Berlin Wall. Brian and I walked over to her smiling, more coherent and more understanding of who we were dealing with and why.

"Hi, Diana," we both said as she smiled faintly. She said nothing. We walked to the doors that led out to the quad. I was still thinking about Jeff. I couldn't help it. I was in shock about the whole thing. I wanted to put him out of my mind. I had to focus on our class assignment, knowing something good would come eventually. I wasn't going to worry why he was dating the Plague. But that strange connection to him felt so real, so incredible.

"So what's on the agenda today, girls?" Brian asked energetically.

"I have to say yesterday was quite an experience. This is turning out to be better than I imagined."

"That's because you didn't have any expectations about what you should experience, Madison," Brian said.

"Well, sometimes I have expectations," I said.

"That's a good way to be," Diana said. There was a long pause of silence. Brian and I looked at her. Did Diana give a compliment? That was the first time I have ever heard Diana say something that was not a negative putdown. We walked to the benches outside the cafeteria as Diana lit a Camel cigarette. She inhaled slowly and then exhaled with relief. As she breathed out, it was as if she was letting go of something painful.

We stood near the benches and my mind went to Jeff again. I tried to think of something else but I couldn't, he had that much of an effect on me. I wanted to let my guard down and ask Brian questions about Jeff. I knew that my aloofness would not have asked him before, but I thought, *What the hell. Screw that damn aloofness. If I'm going to be a reporter I better start practicing my interviewing skills.* I went for the jugular.

"So, Brian, how do you know Jeff?"

"He's my roommate," Brian said matter-of-factly. Of all the people to become experiment partners with, and of all the people to find attractive and have a cosmic connection with, these two people turn out to be roommates. "He was the first person I met here at college and we've been friends ever since. He's a really great guy. He's also the star of the baseball team."

"Yeah, I know." I wanted the dirt. I wanted to know everything about him.

"I didn't know you follow the team. I haven't seen you at the games."

"I don't follow the team really, but I know his girlfriend, Rachel Gibson, and she told me all about it."

"Oh, Rachel." He rolled his eyes slightly and looked away. His tone was not enthusiastic. I could tell he didn't want to get into a conversation about her but I asked anyway.

"Why do you say it like that? Don't you like her?" I asked him. Brian was hesitant to respond; I could tell he didn't like saying a bad thing about anyone. I wondered if he knew that people called her the Plague.

Brian proceeded. "She's okay, she's fine, but…she comes over all the time and doesn't know when it's time to leave."

"Oh, really?" I said. "I could see how that would get annoying especially when you're trying to study."

"It's not that it bothers me but—" He stopped talking. There was silence for a moment. Diana smoked her cigarette as a cool breeze whipped through our jackets.

"I've known Rachel since high school…she means well," I said carefully.

"Oh, yeah, don't get me wrong," Brian said, "she's a very nice girl." Brian looked away. He seemed uncomfortable so I decided to change the subject.

Before I could say anything, Diana put out her cigarette and looked at us inquisitively. "Were you just talking about the baseball team?" she asked.

Brian and I looked at her in surprise and nodded. I had no idea Diana had an interest in what we were discussing or even that she was lending an ear. I didn't think she would be responsive let alone remotely interested in baseball.

"Why do you ask?" I wondered with a raised eyebrow.

She looked at me blankly and said, "I hate the fucking baseball team." Now that was a response I would expect from Diana. Brian turned his head away and put his hand on his chin. He was in deep thought for a moment.

"Diana, what did you say your last name was?" Brian inquired.

"It's Forsythe," she said with a keen snarl. A snarl that penetrated my skin and made me squirm. It was like she utterly despised her last name. There was no pride in her speech. Brian was in deep thought. He scratched the little hair stubble on his chin clearly wishing that he had more facial hair. He had the kind of face that could never achieve a full beard, let alone a five o'clock shadow in the afternoon.

Diana lit up another Camel, taking a drag and exhaling with pleasure. That was the only time I sensed a bit of happiness in Diana. Brian looked at Diana again.

"Hey…no." Brian turned on like a lightbulb, and then abruptly turned off like a switch. His deep blue eyes looked at me and then back at Diana.

"What?" I asked him. "What are you thinking, Brian?"

"I'm not sure," he said.

"What do you mean 'you're not sure'?" I persisted. I felt like I had just grown a set of balls that I didn't have before. I never would have pestered before but now it seemed only right. Brian continued to ponder as Diana took another long drag from her smoke.

"You know, the head coach of the baseball team is Coach Forsythe," Brian stated.

"Oh, is that so?" Diana asked.

"Yes," Brian said matter-of-factly.

I immediately was attentive to Diana and what her expressions had to convey at this point. She took another long drag from the cigarette and exhaled with relief. She looked down at her black combat boots and kicked a pebble on the ground so it went ricocheting off the side of the building. She dropped the cigarette to the ground and stomped on it with her masculine boot. A long hesitation and a loud sigh muffled under her breath.

"He's my father," she said as her dark eyes looked away into the distance.

"The baseball coach is your father?" Brian asked in astonishment.

It didn't seem right, almost not fitting that a father of Diana's could be a coach, a motivator, an encourager, a disciplinarian. It seemed very odd. The two pieces didn't fit. One would think that a coach's daughter would be filled with excitement and enthusiasm about everything because that's what a coach would teach. But somehow that was not the case with Diana. I don't know the man but for Diana to have a coach as a father is like saying a supermodel would have an ugly child.

"How long has your dad been a coach?" I asked her in disbelief.

"All my life," she said, and she kicked another pebble from the sidewalk. "Look, I don't even like sports. I don't like baseball, or jockstraps, or sneakers, or sweat, or running. He's the only reason why I'm even at this stupid school because I get to go here for free because he's the fucking coach." Her voice got loud and rough as it cracked at the pinnacle of her anger.

"Hey, I think it's really cool that your dad's the baseball coach, Diana," I said.

"That's funny, because I don't." She kicked another rock harder this time.

"I need some water, I'll be back." She swung the door wide open as it banged against the side of the building almost shattering the glass. Disgusted, she staggered into the cafeteria. Brian waited until she was fully in the building before turning to me.

"I can't believe her dad's the coach. That seems weird, doesn't it?"

"I know, but we didn't get the full story. Maybe he's her stepfather or adoptive father. We don't know," I said to him.

"Yeah, but it doesn't seem right." He gazed at me.

"I agree," I said as I looked into his blue eyes. Now everything seemed out of character, out of sync, and imbalanced. I looked at Brian and the same uncertainty was going through his face as well.

"Whatever the case may be, there is a lot that must be discovered."

Brian looked at me sternly and said, "I know." Diana came back holding a large bottle of water, taking healthy gulps.

"So are you through talking about me?" Diana said with cynicism.

"We weren't talking about you in a bad way," I said.

"We're just curious, that's all," Brian stated.

"There is really nothing to say other than I had no choice but to come to this school so he could keep an eye on me. Besides he was too damn cheap to send me anyplace else. He lives, breathes, and sleeps baseball; it's nauseating." She was getting really angry.

We started walking through the quad, talking sporadically here and there, but our thoughts were elsewhere. My mind couldn't help but wonder about all the weirdness that had transpired today. First of all, discovering that the only guy I've been attracted to at this school turned out to be Jeff Greenberg. And not only that, but he just happened to be the Plague's boyfriend. Not to mention that he's also Brian's roommate. And now, Diana's father happens to be the coach of the baseball team. And the coach of Jeff, and I'm supposed to go to the game on Saturday. It seems like everything is intertwined but in a very chaotic way. I don't know how all the pieces fit.

We arrived at the pond where many students gathered on nice days to watch the water fountain and enjoy the sun. We sat on the grass and got out our notes about class. Diana hadn't written anything down. Brian, on the other hand, had extensive pages of notes about all that we experienced yesterday. I had written a couple pages, but I think my mental notes were more convincing to me. Somehow seeing what we experienced on paper didn't quit grasp the entire journey.

"How do you think we will be graded for this class?" Brian asked. "The syllabus says that we have three term papers but there is no point structure or grading scale."

"I don't know. I guess he'll assess how well we've grasped these truths. Let's go over them so that we can keep them alive and remember how they transpired. The first one we learned was perceptions of inquiry, then it was forces of nature, and then the ego traits. That's three, we still have six others to experience."

"What do you think the next truth will be? I think it has something to do with the bizarre, and how to unscramble chaos."

"Why do you think that?" Brian asked me, puzzled.

"I don't know," I said. "I just have a hunch."

"I'll tell you what the next truth is. Give me that damn envelope, and I'll make up some crap about one of the sentences written on the paper!" Diana shouted. I actually chuckled at that comment as Brian guarded the manila envelope with his life.

I just didn't understand what was going on. But I had a feeling it was for a greater good. Somehow everything had to come together, but how? I was so confused, so uncertain. I needed to gain some clarity and figure out how everything would fit together. I should recap what I learned yesterday and hopefully I could make some sense of it.

I knew that from my "perceptions about gaining knowledge" truth, I shouldn't judge what is happening or come to any false sense of closure. The "forces of nature" truth taught me that I must stay neutral by not having any preconceived notions or expectations. And from the "ego trait" truth, I learned that I must let go of my aloofness. I must not be afraid to speak my mind and ask questions that will help me reach a better understanding by gaining the necessary knowledge that I need to move on.

Now, I just found out some amazing discoveries about the people around me and I didn't know how to make sense of it all. I took a deep breath and let the energy of the beautiful tranquil environment seep into my mind, body, and soul. I had to really inhale all the freshness of the air, and breathe in the energy from the large trees. I needed to feel the power of the sun's light on my face. The three of us sat by the pond just breathing. The silence was golden.

After a few minutes of reflection, Brian took a small rock from the side of the pond and side-armed it into the water causing it to skip. It skimmed across the top of the water and then hopped through the slow rippling current and over the ducks that were basking in the warm sun.

He repeated this motion getting more and more entertained by how many times he could make the rock skip. At first it skipped twice. Then he would windup and put a little more gusto into his side-arm motion and slowly the rock skipped three times. It took very little to keep Brian entertained and he was happy. Diana watched him as she smoked more cigarettes and sketched something with ink in her notebook. I couldn't get over the sight of Jeff, but most of all I couldn't get over that he was dating the Plague.

It was around four o'clock and the sun was getting lower making the water glisten like sparkling glitter. The pond looked beautiful and peaceful as joggers ran along and walkers strolled hand in hand. The sunbathers were reading literature or newspapers, and some students were actually working on their assignments. I was too confused to concentrate on anything so I sat perched on the grass holding my knees in my arms. I was simply breathing in and out. One of the joggers was finishing his work out as he slowed down his pace and looked at his watch that was keeping time and tracking his distance. He grabbed hold of his thin wrist and began counting slowly to himself. As sweat beads dribbled down the side of his square jawline, he mouthed the numbers but not directly saying them aloud. His face was slightly clenched from the pain in his chest, while trying to slow down his heavy panting. The more I looked at him I thought he looked familiar to me. Was he a professor I had before? He looked like my high school science teacher, tall and lanky with wiry limbs, thinning hair, and a red mustache. For a moment, I was tempted to ask him if he was, in fact, Mr. Eberwiess, but no…it wasn't him. I had never seen this man before. But I felt that I needed to talk to him.

Brian stopped his rock skipping for a moment as he noticed the jogger breathing heavily nearby. "Hey, buddy, do you need some water?" The jogger motioned to him that he was all right, waving his arm.

"No, I'm fine. I haven't run three miles in months and I'm trying to get back into shape. I used to run a lot more," he said while still trying to catch his breath. He walked around slowly while holding the side of his rib cage. He continued to walk off his pain. I sympathized with him, knowing that feeling of your heart pounding so fast you think you're going to die and you can't feel your legs because they're like Jell-O.

I sat watching him as many thoughts sped through my mind. I realized that my mind was feeling total chaos.

The jogger sat down on a wooden bench adjacent to us as he let out a loud groan. I watched as the perspiration trickled down his face and his rosy cheeks puffed in and out. His heavy breathing had slowly subsided as he gazed upon the beautiful pond. The sun was starting its descent in the west behind the lavish oak trees in the backdrop. He looked at the pond in admiration as his face shone brightly. He appeared blissful and proud, as if his entire body was beaming. He was glowing with extraordinary delight. He had a sense of accomplishment about him that seemed to say, "I did it."

The great Winston Churchill once said, "If you're going through hell, keep going." During the jogger's run, he probably felt that his body was going through hell, but he kept on going. And now, for having gone through that hell, he was filled with a beautiful euphoria of mind, body, and soul. A blissful rejuvenation was taking place. The running had cleansed his body from the negative impurities that were living inside, as the brain's level of serotonin increased creating a "high" of profound magnitude that cannot fully be described, only felt.

I took large breaths and tried to inhale all the energy from the gorgeous surroundings. I tried to think of peace and calm. I closed my eyes and tried to picture feeling the high of the jogger. But I couldn't, I was too confused. The jogger began breathing normally as he looked at the three of us with a transparent light in his eye. He was vibrantly alive. And then it dawned on me that the mind and body go through many forms of chaos, but when they eventually settle down and breathe in the energy of the universe they end up feeling more alive and more rejuvenated.

"It's nice seeing college students enjoying their surroundings and appreciating their campus," he remarked.

I didn't hesitate to answer him. "Yes, this pond is really great." I looked at him and then at the pond. "It looks like you got a great workout."

"Yeah, I'm training for a 10k run that is coming up in two months and I really need to get back in shape. I was having a hard time there at the end of my run, but I feel much better now.

"It's always a great feeling after the fact, isn't it?" I asked.

"That's so true." He looked at me deeply for a moment, then took a few sips of water from the bottle and let out a sigh. I was looking at him but thinking of Jeff and the Plague, and Diana and the baseball game, and everything. It swirled together.

"It looks like you have a lot on your mind; do you have a test coming up?"

"If you mean an academic test no, but…"

"Ah, you have other life tests that are going on…I see." He spoke articulately, as if his mind was so clear that he came up with the right words to say at exactly the right moment. I felt like I could be open with him.

"It was just one of those days when everything gets thrown at you at once and you're not sure what to think. It's overwhelming. He looked at me as if he knew exactly what I was talking about, like he understood completely.

"There is no problem then," he said matter-of-factly.

"What do you mean?" I asked him. "There are major problems going on and I don't know how to make sense of them."

"You don't have to make sense of them," he said as he sipped more water.

"What do you mean?" I demanded.

"The truth is always misunderstood." He looked at me. "There are many factors involved when it comes to fully understanding a situation and why it is happening to you. First, let me explain to you that when situations arise, you must interpret them correctly by not making any wrong judgments or rash conclusions without knowing the full story."

"I know that. I learned the perceptions of human inquiry and why they are vital when gaining knowledge about the world." The jogger looked surprised.

"I'm in Dr. Nolan's philosophy class," I explained. I had a feeling he would know about the class.

"Actually all three of us are in the class." I pointed toward Diana and Brian. They walked over near the jogger and me.

"I'm Madison, and that's Brian and Diana."

"So you all have a solid understanding of how we gain knowledge, of the forces that govern us, and about egos? And do you also understand that the coincidences that happen are meant for a reason, to lead us into the right direction?"

"Yes, we learned about them the other day. Now we are at a point where we are trying to make sense of everything and we're so confused."

The jogger nodded at me and then proceeded. "The truth is always misunderstood. By that, I mean at first you won't know exactly why something is happening until you have figured out the right question."

"I don't think you understand us," Brian said. "We are asking questions to get the right answer."

"Yes, you are looking for the answers, but you must know that in order to find the answers you must ask the right questions. You must realize that at first the truth is misunderstood, because we all need to be tested about out beliefs. Think about it. If you were never tested on your beliefs, how could you really know if they are real? How could you ever learn about yourself? That is why we need to be tested so that we can understand our situation more clearly and understand our beliefs more clearly. We all have our life story and this story is moving along on a path, and whether you realize it or not everything that has happened to you leading up to this very moment is part of your own divine life plan. This plan has been derived even before our birth. We all have a life question that is at the core of our existence but you must discover that question before you find the answers. To find the answers you must discover your life question."

"So what are you saying?" Brian asked. "To find the answers to a particular situation we must be asking ourselves the right question?"

"Yes," the jogger said. "That's right."

"How do we know what our life question is?" I asked.

68

"You will learn it when you are ready. But first, you must value that the 'truth,' no matter what you might think it is, is always misunderstood. In any particular situation, you never fully know the truth because there are three sides to every story, your side, the other side, and the right side. The right side or the 'truth' is something we almost never interpret correctly because after we have exhausted all of the possible conclusions that we can muster in our minds, there is still something we cannot see, or something we cannot discover because we have yet to ask the right question. This question is at the center of our life at all times. But we are often so far away from our life question that most people never figure out what it is. This question is that innate force that drives us, it's what makes us get up in the morning, it's that little tickle in your throat right before you sneeze. Some people call it their life dream; some call it a personal calling; other call it their purpose for living."

"But most people are not on this same wavelength. How can we get them to understand us?" I asked.

"The truth is always misunderstood. Just remember that, Madison."

Truth #4—*The truth is always misunderstood. By not fully understanding the "truth," this forces us to be more introspective and thus allows our spirit to grow.*

I sat and pondered those words for a minute. My body began to feel lighter again and more alive.

"Why can't we understand it?" Diana asked him.

"Because people are not advanced enough, they think on a surface-level plane. They do not delve deeper into a particular situation. They merely rationalize a situation, make a judgment, a snap conclusion, and then stick to that conclusion regardless if it really is right."

"That was what we learned about in our perceptions truth," Diana said.

"Right, do you see how that works here?" We all nodded at the jogger.

"What are we lacking that will help us understand the truth? And not let it be misunderstood? How do we discover our life question?" I asked him desperately.

"I will tell you," he said. "There have been so many times in the past I've felt misunderstood by others and wondered why. But now I know that to be misunderstood by others is essential when trying to find your truth. Because being misunderstood by others makes you grow as a person and the very opposition will help validate your own truth to yourself. As I said before, if we are never tested on what we stand for, how can we validate our beliefs?"

As I sat pondering, I immediately thought of Jesus Christ and how his entire being was truth. He was misunderstood by others his entire life. In fact, he is still misunderstood today. The reason he was so misunderstood was because of the people's egos at the time.

In the midst of my thinking, the jogger interrupted. "Misunderstandings and ego traits go hand in hand. If we learn to drop our ego traits we can achieve our truth. However, we can only achieve our true self by having full energy."

We all listened closely to the jogger. I reflected on relationships I had with friends and family members, and how completely misunderstood I felt at times when we would have arguments. The reason I was misunderstood was because our energy levels and egos were actually fighting each other to feel better and gain energy. It was becoming clearer now.

"How can we learn to understand the truth and ask the right question?" I asked the jogger.

"Be patient, Madison, I'll explain."

*The smallest fact is a window
through which the infinite may be seen.*
—Aldous Huxley

VII

THE THIRD EYE

We all looked at the jogger, wondering what he would say next. He paused for a long moment trying to collect his thoughts.

"You must recognize that what you think is true is often not and you must correlate that knowledge with your own life question. You will learn about your life question when you are ready. I'm here to teach you that when you feel your world is chaotic the way to make sense of things is to count on your third eye."

"What? Third eye?" Diana asked. "The last time I checked, I only have two eyes, and they are enough for me."

The jogger laughed. "The third eye is not to be taken literally. It is there spiritually, and it acts as your guide. Think of it as your window into the infinite. This third eye is intuitive and its wisdom is remarkable. The third eye encompasses three basic principles. Together these basic principles make up a third eye. The principles are about your instincts, your thoughts, and your dreams. Think of yourself as having a giant eye in the middle of your forehead that is there to guide at all times. It's there to see things in a different light that ordinarily would never been seen. It is there to help you change your perceptions, and if you change your perceptions then your outcomes will change. But it will only appear when you are connected to its source and when you have dropped your ego.

"If you are not connected to the source of the universe, and your ego is interfering, your third eye will not work for you. The third eye will help you be true to your instincts, but you must be keen to your instincts and intuition to let your third eye guide you. The only way to be connected to the third eye is to stay connected to the source of the universe."

"I'm very keen on my premonitions, and also on my thoughts and dreams," I told him.

"That's good, Madison. But it's one thing to be aware of them sometimes, but when you bring them fully into your conscious world you make them real, and they are no longer dreams of the subconscious, they become your reality. You must give them the power that they deserve and not overlook them as having little or no significance, because they do. Your instincts, premonitions, and daydreams arise to lead you into the right path. They carry the messages that are integral to your life question.

"The first principle of the third eye pertains to your instincts. Your instincts are very powerful and they can lead you to great discoveries. This is relevant when you see someone or something stand out to you for some reason, and even though you have never seen them before, they look familiar to you. Your instincts are telling you that you should talk to that person because they have a message for you that will help you reach a higher plateau. Have you ever experienced that before?"

"Yes, in fact, as I saw you finishing your run, I thought you were my old science teacher. You looked very familiar to me and I instinctively knew you had something to contribute but I didn't know what."

The jogger's eyes lit up. "See, your instincts were telling you I had a message for you; a message that would help you move in the direction that you need to go."

"What about you?" He looked toward Diana.

"I had a premonition that this philosophy class would change me somehow, but I had no idea how, and I still have no idea why. Maybe that was why I was scared of it at first. I even wanted to drop the class because I was frightened about what I would learn and experience," she admitted.

"Well, everything you experience changes you one way or another," he pointed out. "Let me remind you of the forces of nature that you have already learned. When you go into a situation as neutral by not having preconceived notions either positive or negative, you then perceive the situation in a way that opens your eyes. When you are open, you gain clarity.

"What I mean by clarity is that you begin to understand that you are experiencing something profound, and your mind and body become filled with energy, thus making your mind clear. Once you reach this clarity, you must follow your instincts, your thoughts, and your dreams to give you messages that lead you in the right direction. But it is imperative that you first recognize the coincidences, then change your perceptions, become neutral and clear, and drop your ego. Once you accomplish that, you must use your third eye to sort through the obstacles to help you understand why things are occurring."

"So the third eye consists of your instincts, thoughts, and dreams?" Brian asked.

"Yes, that is why it is a third eye. It's an intuitive eye. It delves deeper into situations. By following your third eye you will then have to ask the appropriate questions that lead you to your core question, as it is often referred to. Your core question is the most important question you need to ask and when you discover this question you will achieve true clarity. In order to find your core question you must utilize your third eye and all of its mystery. You must make it your friend, and make it a part of you. But you must recognize it is there to help you."

He continued. "Somehow, everything gets lost when we fail to recognize the coincidences that occur. What usually happens when we recognize and discover that somehow your best friend is related to your boss, or that your neighbor is your coworker's relative? We usually think that's just bizarre, but that coincidence is trying to tell you something to make your life grow. Sometimes we might even run into someone twice in one week and say, 'Oh, funny seeing you again.' We don't delve deeper into the situation to discover that this person has a message for us or that you must have something to learn from the coincidence. We usually shrug it off as being purely left to chance, or luck, or just downright weird." I nodded my head. I had many coincidences happen in the past but I could never make sense of why they were happening.

"Once you start recognizing the coincidences, you then must truly understand the ways we gain knowledge about the world and we must alter our perceptions and remember the forces of nature by maintaining neutrality. Then you must drop your ego trait, and then learn to use your third eye of instinct, thoughts, and dreams to make the coincidences occur more frequently so that you can reach your answers quickly. That will speed up the process and move your life into the direction that your were destined to live. Our journey here is spiritual and is based on gaining knowledge."

He paused while looking at each of us closely.

"So do you all understand instincts and how they work?"

"Yes. You must follow your gut feeling, right? And not question it?" I asked.

"That's right, you must always go with what you think. Even if you think it turned out to be the wrong decision at the time, it was always the right one for you all along."

Brian was skeptical. "Wait," he said. "Even if you went with your instinct at a particular moment and you thought it was the wrong decision after the fact, it was actually the right one all along?"

"Yes, does that make sense?" he asked. "Sometimes your gut feelings lead you into a situation that you might feel is off your plan, or not quite right. But in actuality, your gut feeling was always part of the plan. You might think that it was wrong because you ended up in a painful situation that ended up causing you problems. The reason you had to endure that hurt was because at that particular time you had to learn a valuable lesson, and from that lesson your spirit was able to grow. That pain was what you needed at the time. But at the moment you didn't understand that concept, all you could think of was the pain you felt. But your plan was teaching you more patience, or more independence, or to be more appreciative, and you had to learn that. You were enduring that particular painful situation at that time to reach a higher synthesis or higher level of thinking, and a better understanding of yourself and the world. Your instincts are always right and to follow them means being on your chosen path.

"Can you think of an example of following your instincts?" the jogger asked Brian.

Brian began to think and after much hesitation he began to speak. "I can think of a time when an instinct helped me avoid a dangerous situation. I was driving in the car with my father. The car was loaded up with all my belongings as my father was helping me move into school here. We were driving along on the interstate highway, and we were talking and listening to music, as my father had the cruise control set at seventy miles per hour. I was pretty nervous about starting college, and I remember the exact conversation that my father and I were having. I was asking my dad if he thought I was making the right decision by going to college at this university. He reassured me that I was making the right decision, and told me about the terrific biology program that I was to attend. But I still didn't believe him one hundred percent. I was still unsure.

"We proceeded to drive along in the right lane of traffic. We eventually drove up behind a slow-moving truck that was hauling large boulders in the back. We were chatting about my school decision and not paying much attention. I suddenly noticed the truck had gone over a pot-hole in the road causing the boulders in the back of the truck to move slightly. I instinctively told my father that he should change lanes and pass the truck on the left. My dad looked at me and put his signal on to get over to the left lane. As we sped by the truck, my father was still looking in his rearview mirror. To his surprise a massive boulder fell off the back of the truck and onto the road. I turned my head back and saw the boulder fall onto the highway.

"If my instincts didn't tell me at that precise moment to tell my father to change lanes, we surely would have been crushed to death by the boulders. My dad and I never spoke of that moment again, but I know he still thinks about it. I can still hear it in his voice every so often."

"Wow," the jogger said. We all looked at Brian in amazement.

"That is extraordinary," I said, as chills ran down my spine.

Brian's eyes became moist. "From that day on, I knew that I belonged at college here, somehow I was destined to be here and nothing was going to stop me, otherwise we would have never made it." Brian's voice cracked and he looked away. He was emotional, as I put my hand on his shoulder and warmly smiled at him.

"Do you understand what happened?" the jogger proceeded. "You were asking a very important question about whether or not you made the right decision, and your third eye of instinct solidified that indeed you were making the right decision. The mystical aspect is that, it answered your question at the exact moment you were asking it. You sent out a message to the universe that you were unsure of your decision to attend this college, and then your third eye spoke to you by instinctively telling you to change lanes. If you didn't listen to your third eye, you might not have lived to tell us that miraculous story."

The jogger cleared his throat and went on. "I'll give you another example of instincts of the third eye," he said. "Let's say that someone very dear to you has recently passed on. Because you feel you've lost your sense of self, you become completely depressed, not wanting to get out of bed, hardly able to perform the daily activities of life. Your energy has sunk to its lowest point ever, and you are not sure if you can carry on. Due to your depression, your personal hygiene is suffering. Even the simplest tasks such as brushing your teeth have become a chore. You desperately try to make it to the store to get some personal care items that you need.

"You stagger around the supermarket in a daze, and like a walking zombie you eventually make it to the checkout counter. There is a long line of people with hundreds of items before you waiting to pay for their groceries. You huff and puff to yourself in despair, as the few items you're holding are like heavy weights in your arms. You realize that you have no patience for the checkout line you're in. You look over to the other checkout line and it seems to pop out at you. It appears more vibrant and more welcoming than the line you are in. You move out of that line into the other. You have a feeling it will move quicker than the last. You wait a few moments in the line and finally make it to the cashier. The cashier greets you with a hello and a smile. She looks straight into your eyes and says, 'How are you, today?' She must ask that question to hundreds of customers every day, but this time she is genuinely concerned, because she can sense the utter isolation in your face.

"You look up from your money counting and say, 'I'm fine.' She continues to beam a beautiful smile of peace and solitude toward you. She projects her energy into you as you look at her. Her smile is as bright as the sun. You suddenly start to feel a little bit better, because her smile and warm regards are uplifting you and giving you energy. She gives you back your change, her sparkling eyes radiating into yours, and says, 'Don't worry, time heals all wounds.' Those words bandage your wounded heart. They are calming and soothing to your tormented suffering soul. All you can do is look at her and shrug your shoulders and say, 'Thank you.'"

The jogger paused and looked at us. We were listening very carefully. "Those were exactly the words you needed to hear at that particular moment to carry on. You needed to know that there was hope, that there was light at the end of the tunnel. To know that someone else understood, could sympathize, and being a complete stranger made it even more meaningful. You walk out of the grocery store feeling lighter, but still not quite the same old you. As you walk out the door holding two heavy grocery bags in your hands, a man helps you carry your bags to the car. You smile knowing that someone else is willing to hold your baggage for a short time. You feel even lighter and better.

"As you get in the car and start driving, your favorite song comes on the radio. It fills you with thoughts of happier times. It immediately uplifts your spirit even more, and it reminds you of good times and memories of happiness. As you continue to drive, you sense your old self coming back a little. You even smile for the first time in weeks. And it's all because you had the instinct to go to the other checkout line as opposed to the one you were originally at in the first place. The cashier had started a snowball effect of good things to come, and it was all because she took an unselfish moment out of her day to give you energy and uplift your spirit. If you had avoided your instinct and stayed in the first line, you would have missed an opportunity to slowly come out of your depression. That is why your instincts are so important. Let them guide you in times of trouble, and in times of happiness."

As the jogger told his story, I thought of how the coincidences of happy occurrences happened in threes. First the friendly cashier, then the man that helped with the bags, then the favorite song came on the radio.

"Does the third eye have something to do with the number three?" I asked the jogger.

"Yes, I'm glad you picked up on that. Obviously, because it is your third eye that consists of three principles—your instincts, your thoughts, and your dreams—there is a definite parallel to the number three. Largely because the number three symbolizes the trinity. The Father, Son, and the Holy Spirit. The third eye is there in the Holy Spirit form because the three principles of the third eye are spiritual in nature. The mystical and mysterious Holy Spirit comes to guide us with the ever-present third eye."

"That is really interesting," Brian said, as he focused on the knowledgeable jogger.

"What about our thoughts? How do they lead us in the right direction?" Diana wondered.

"Well, the thoughts and premonitions you have about the future are strongly related to the questions that you have," the jogger explained.

"I don't get it. You mean our core question?" I asked.

"Your core question is the big question of what your true purpose is. But your other questions are the smaller ones that lead up to the larger question. Does that make sense?"

The jogger looked at us as we stared at him, puzzled.

"Okay, let me give you an example of how your thoughts guide you. Let's say you have a big final coming up for your calculus class. Throughout the entire semester you were having trouble with the material. You asked the professor for help and you even got a tutor for more practice. You still could only grasp the bare minimum of the subject matter. No matter how much you studied or how much you tried to understand it, you were completely lost. It just didn't sink in. You found yourself two weeks before the final exam failing the class.

"The failing was not because of your lack of effort. You simply couldn't get the right answers. You thought you were following the appropriate steps, performing the right techniques, but you were still doing something terribly wrong and didn't know what. When you would ask the professor for more help, it appeared he didn't want to spend the extra time with you. He looked at you as a lost cause. You didn't know which way to turn. You asked your tutor, your friends, even your family for help and they tried the best they could. It was now up to you to come up with the right answers.

"Still attempting the problems and working through them your answers always came up wrong. You finally thought 'I'll never get it. I'm just stupid. Calculus and I just don't mix. I give up. I'll just step away from it for two days and see what happens.' You go about your other activities for two days and try not to even think about calculus. You study your other subjects, have fun with friends, and never think about calculus.

"But one night as you're laying your head down to go to sleep, eyes closed, seeing many shapes and designs in the darkness, many thoughts go through your head. You start to feel anxiety knowing that you need to pass this calculus class as part of your major's core requirements, and if you don't pass this course you won't fulfill your requirements to graduate. And if you don't graduate you'll never be able to fulfill the career path that you've worked so hard for. You bounce around the question, 'What am I doing wrong?' You think that by saying it aloud, a voice might come down to tell you the answer. You wait for a minute, but you hear nothing, no voice, no answer.

"You calm down, relax your body, breath in and out, and focus on sleeping. You try to relax your mind to just concentrate on sleep. Then you start seeing numbers, plus and minus signs, parentheses, as you begin working out a calculus problem in your head. Without an open book, or pencil, the problem was coming to life in your mind. You perform the FOIL method in your head. You know you had mastered that technique. In your mind you worked through the rest of the problem. Then you realized that you were not multiplying the result of the parenthesis and dividing by the coefficient. Instead you were multiplying by the coefficient—that was why your answers were always wrong. It was like a lightbulb in your head.

"You jump out of bed and immediately open your calculus book and work out the problems with this newfound knowledge that you received. Sure enough, your thoughts were right. You work through the problems and check your answers in the back of the book. Every problem you attempted came out to be the right answer. You couldn't believe it. Just when you were at the point of giving up, your thoughts led you to discover the right answers after all."

"That's amazing." Brian said. "That has happened to me a couple of times, but I don't quite remember them now."

"Wow!" Diana and I looked at the jogger in wonderment.

"So you have to ask a question and it will come?" I asked. "It sounds too easy."

"No, it's not that easy. You have to disassociate yourself from the problem and gain clarity by breathing in the energy of the universe, by utilizing all of the other truths that you have learned to achieve the right answer."

"What about our dreams?" I asked wanting to know everything this man had to say. "What do they teach us?" I've always tried to figure out my dreams but they never made sense. And most of the time I could never remember them. I told the jogger.

"It's important to condition your mind to remember them because dreams run parallel to your life. When analyzed correctly they can answer questions that guide your path.

"What about nightmares?" Diana wondered.

"Bad dreams have the most profound messages," the jogger insisted.

"Really? But how do we interpret them?" Brian asked inquisitively.

"You have to compare parts of the dream to your life. Have any of you had a dream recently that you could share with us? The jogger looked at all three of us as we stared back at him. We thought for a moment.

Diana responded, "I had a nightmare yesterday morning that really scared me.

"Was it the morning of the first day of class?" the jogger asked.

"Yeah, actually it was right before I was woken up by the alarm clock. I still remember it very well."

"Let me help you interpret it," the jogger replied eagerly.

"Where should I start?" Diana wondered.

"At the beginning, always start at the beginning."

Diana went on. "My father and I were driving in my car and we were completely lost on a deserted road. My dad was driving and I was in the passenger's seat. It was dark and it was pouring rain. The rain was coming down so fast we could barely see a foot in front of us. The rain kept crashing down on the car as the windshield wipers tried to keep up with all the water."

"How did you feel?" the jogger asked her.

"I felt terrified. The rain was overwhelming and it just kept coming down heavy and fast.

"Compare that situation to your life right now. Are you feeling lost, scared, and overwhelmed?"

"Yes, I have five classes this semester, and I'm not sure if I have an interest in any of them. The workload is too much and I don't think this is the major I want to pursue. I didn't even want to come to this school, but my father made me because he has been the baseball coach here for twenty-two years."

"Oh, that's why he is driving the car. He has the control and you feel like a passenger in your own life. Is that right?" the jogger analyzed.

"Yeah, I guess," Diana responded.

"So what happened then?" he asked.

"We eventually came to a bridge. I told my dad to go over the bridge so we could get to the other side. It wasn't raining on the other side of the bridge. My father refused to go over the bridge, but I kept insisting.

So he started slowly driving over the bridge as the rain continued to crash down."

"Then what?" he inquired.

"Suddenly, as we were driving on the bridge, the bridge opened up and the car fell into the high river and we began sinking in the water. The entire car was being swallowed by the river. We were both horrified. Then I woke up."

"Okay, stop right there," the jogger ordered. "So you are feeling lost and overwhelmed. You feel as if your dad is holding the wheel of your life and he is driving you to crash. What does the bridge symbolize to you?"

"A way to get to the other side, where there is no rain," Diana said.

"No, actually, the bridge is your connection with your father, and you feel as if it's broken or fallen apart. Hence, the bridge opening up and leading you and your father to be swallowed by the river."

"What about the other side? There was no rain on the other side. Why? Why couldn't I get there?" Diana was becoming angry.

"The other side was not where you needed to be, you need to be dealing with the rain on this side of the bridge. You're not quit over the rain to reach the other side, the drier side. You need to deal with the present rain." The jogger looked at her with compassion.

"So I shouldn't be thinking 'what if'? Or wondering about other possibilities?" Diana asked him with frustration.

"That's right, you are exactly where you need to be, dealing with the rain. Eventually, you will get to the other side."

"How? When can I get to the other side?" Diana asked passionately. The jogger said nothing. There was a long pause. Diana grew frustrated with him. "I need to fix the bridge, right? By fixing the bridge?"

The jogger looked at her and said, "I didn't say that; you did. See, you thought that going to the other side of the bridge would solve all your problems and worry. But right now you need to deal with the here and now, take one day at a time, and work on fixing your relationship with your father. If you do that, you will find a new insight of who you are as a person and what you should do with your life. You might think that your father is holding you back, but really you are the one that is holding yourself back."

Diana sat on the wooden bench and took a deep breath, as the jogger, Brian, and I looked at her with empathy. She gazed out onto the pond in thought.

"I hope this helps you understand what the dream meant and how it's parallel to your current life situation." Diana slowly turned her head to him and said, "Thank you." She was sincere and kind. I saw a side of her that I didn't know existed.

"It is so important that you all recognize the three principles of the third eye. Your instincts, your thoughts, and your dreams will always guide you and give you messages that steer you in the right direction."

Truth #5—*We all have a third eye. It consists of your instincts, your thoughts, and your dreams. Your third eye will guide you and give you messages that steer you in the right direction.*

"What about finding our core question to ask?" I wondered. "How do we know if we are asking the right question?"

"You will learn about that when you are ready." The jogger looked at his watch and gathered his water bottle from the wooden bench. "I really must be going, if I miss dinner, my wife will be upset. It was nice talking to you three, and just remember to listen to your third eye. It is there to help you."

We thanked the jogger and smiled at him.

"Good luck with your training," I said as he walked away.

"Good luck to you with the class," he said, winking at us.

Brian was excited about the conversation.

"That was really cool that he interpreted your dream like that, Diana."

"Yeah, it was," she said in a low voice.

"What do you think you need to do about your father?" I asked her.

She took another deep breath. "I don't know, I just don't know." She looked away.

"I'm sure you'll figure it out." I put my hand on her shoulder, and it was strange that I felt comfortable enough to show her affection. Diana didn't reject it either. She was slowly letting down her wall and widening her bridge with us. She was allowing herself to experience the beauty of communication. I got the feeling she wasn't very familiar with that concept. I felt proud of her in a way. The three of us looked at each other and smiled for a moment as the sun hung low in the backdrop. I looked into the large manila envelope that Dr. Jacobs had given us from class. I put my hand inside, and I pulled out the next ticket. I read it aloud. It said, "Messages from the third eye."

"Cool! We have now uncovered five truths. Each one more amazing and more enlightening. What do you think the next one is?" Brian wondered.

"We will see. We shall see," Diana said.

If you bury your dreams
you bury gold.

—Euripedes

VIII

THE CORE

I woke up in confusion. The discoveries I made about Jeff and the Plague, as well as Diana and her father, were still on my mind. I could not fathom why the only man I was attracted to was dating the one person I despised. It seemed that everything I had encountered lately was interconnected.

I felt like I was on a dizzying carousel ride, riding a bright, colorful horse. It was a strange ride, going up and down and around and around. The carousel was taking me on its own journey and I felt like a bag of mixed nuts.

I realized that in order to find out why all of this was happening, I had to remember my third eye and use it to guide me to discover the other truths. The past three days, I had learned the way we gain knowledge and perceive knowledge; positive, negative and neutral signs of energy; ego traits; why we need to be misunderstood; and the third eye. Each truth signified all the different aspects of me. Even though I was really confused, it didn't bother me. I almost welcomed it.

I opened the blinds to let some light in the vintage kitchen. Flying dust particles shimmered in the air, as soft light reflected onto the white linoleum floor. It had rained overnight and there were little beads of water on the window as I noticed the strong oak tree weeping water from its leaves. Even with the blinds open the kitchen was dark and gloomy.

I made my way to the counter and peeled a large ripe banana from the fruit bowl. I put coffee in the coffeemaker, got out the cream and sugar, and perched myself on one of our rickety kitchen chairs. My roommate Victoria and I always prided ourselves in making the apartment look trendy and stylish on a shoestring budget. We called it flashy trash. If it meant going to consignment shops, garage sales, and flea markets, we were there. We were like two old ladies shopping in our do-rags, slippers, and oversized purses, picking out knickknacks and checking them out thoroughly for small imperfections. We were like Lucy and Ethel. I was Lucy, the one with some crazy, scheming idea, and she was Ethel, the one who always went along with it.

Victoria should be waking up soon. She was not much of a morning person, especially before she'd had her coffee and cereal. Every morning we ate breakfast together in a rush, always recapping what had happened the night before and general girly gossipy stuff.

I continued to eat my banana, slowly unraveling the skin, and taking little bites, piece by piece, examining all the intricate details: its lines, its ridges, its textures. A banana is complex perfection. To eventually reach the beautiful, tasteful, splendor of this perfection you must keep unraveling and disentangling the skin to get to the core of its magnificence. When you reach the core, you can consume its brilliance.

All of God's gifts to us are internal or hidden deep inside a shell. Even the smallest nut has layers of skin that must be discarded before you reach the core. All of the important, meaty pieces are inside. At that moment the banana was the most precious thing in the world to me.

Victoria wiped the sleep out of her eyes and brushed her auburn hair off her face as she walked into the bathroom. Three minutes later she was in the kitchen.

"What's up, Vic?" I asked.

"I'm tired. This semester is kicking my ass. I already have a paper due tomorrow."

"For which class?"

"Teaching methods of secondary education; it's all about various teaching methods."

"That sounds pretty interesting."

"Yeah, but it's actually kind of boring."

"Where's the Cocoa Pebbles?" She gave me a look, hoping there were some left.

"In the cabinet to your right," I pointed.

Victoria got out a bowl and filled it to the rim with cereal. She poured skim milk, causing the cereal to overflow onto the countertop. She bent down and slurped off the top layer of cereal from the bowl with her mouth then carefully carried the bowl to the table trying not to spill it on the floor. She sat down on the rickety chair next to me, chewing loudly. Chomp, chomp, chomp. Sometimes it was the little things that got under your skin, but after a while those idiosyncracies become the beauty you saw in a person.

"So what's new with you?" she asked with a full mouth.

"Oh my God, I have so much to tell you. This philosophy class is turning out to be really bizarre. I told you how we have to discover nine truths, right?"

"Yeah, have you discovered any yet?"

"That's the weird thing. We've already discovered five of them, and they have been so interesting that I can't even begin to describe to you how cool this whole thing is turning out."

"How do you like your partners? How's the bitchy girl? Is she still in your group?"

"Yeah, she is, and I'm learning a lot about her."

"Like what?"

"Her father is the baseball coach. And guess who he's coaching?"

"Who?" she looked at me wide-eyed.

"Jeff Greenberg, you know the Plague's boyfriend?"

"Yeah…and…?"

"Well, I met him yesterday; he's also Brian's roommate and he's really cute."

"Do you like him?"

"I don't know. How could I like him when he's dating her?"

"Stranger things have happened."

FIRST CLASS TICKET

I sat silent for a moment as Victoria ate the rest of her cereal. She got to the bottom of the bowl and drank a pool of chocolate milk. She slurped it up with satisfaction.

"So what truth are you on now?" she asked.

"I'm not sure, but I think it has something to do with our core question."

"What's that?"

"What we're supposed to do with our lives—why are we here, what is our purpose?"

"That's way too deep for me."

"Vic, let me ask you—were your parents disappointed when you told them that you didn't want to pursue the piano anymore?"

"Yeah, they were really upset for a long time, but they eventually got over it. Especially after I explained to them over and over again that I would rather teach people than perform for people. They always had this expectation for me to become a famous classical pianist. I never wanted to be famous or well known. I just want a simple life. I didn't want all that traveling in different cities every night, living out of a suitcase, and hotel rooms, different beds without sleep. I didn't want paparazzi, or spotlights, or harsh reviews, or critiques.

"I'll be happy being a music teacher at a high school or college, with my summers off and weekends free. I'll still be doing what I love, which is music, but not in the way they wanted. It's not in me to be a constant performer. I would rather perform for students who really need to learn, rather than perform for an audience whose only need is to be entertained. I'm a teacher, not an entertainer."

"How did you realize that?" I asked her.

"When I was entertaining, I didn't like who I was, or what I was becoming. I didn't feel like myself. Why do you ask? Are you thinking of giving up journalism?"

"No, no, I love journalism. I'm not giving it up. I was just curious how you knew that teaching was the right path for you."

Victoria looked at me and smiled. I crumpled up a napkin and threw it in her face; she threw it back, hitting me smack in the nose.

88

Then the phone rang loudly. Victoria jumped to answer it. It was probably one of her boyfriends.

The story of how Victoria and I become friends is really quite interesting.

When I was a child and later into my teens, I was an avid pianist just like Victoria. The piano danced when I played it. It was like my hands had the power to make the piano alive. I loved the piano and it loved me. During my senior year of high school, I wasn't sure if I should go to Juilliard to pursue the piano, or go to school here to become a journalist. I was feeling restless about which direction my life should go. I desperately needed some reassurance so I decided to see an old familiar face, my old piano teacher Mr. Stein.

Mr. Stein was an elderly man with glasses, a long white beard, and a round belly. He was humble and soft-spoken, and reminded me of Santa Claus. He was warm and gentle, and easy to talk to. We chatted for a while in the old classroom in the basement of the Steinway store on the Upper West Side. The room always smelled of Ben-Gay. The old fan was blowing, and the dust particles on the blades were as thick and gray as Stein's beard. The old familiar brown and white tile floor still bore the same scratch marks, and he still had those old untouched Hershey kisses in a crystal bowl beside the piano. I looked at his displays on the wall, and noticed the same picture of Uncle Sam pointing at me saying, *I want* you *to practice every day.* The fire in Uncle Sam's eye had faded over the years now, but Mr. Stein still possessed his charm. It felt great to be back in that stale room, where I first learned the acronyms of Every Good Boy Deserves Fudge, and how All Cars Eat Gas, of scales, and staccatos, and tempos, and four-four time, piano recitals, Beethoven, and his favorite, Bach.

We caught up on everything. He was probably the most influential person in my life. He had old-school wisdom. He taught me piano lessons as well as life lessons. From him, I learned that life imitates art and how art imitates life. Each music piece and every movement in the music become the movements of life. Some fast, some slow, some happy, some sad, some dark, some moody—others bright and alive. He made me recognize this.

Whenever, I would get frustrated on a certain piece he would settle me down and tell me, "If you close your eyes you can feel the music." At first, I didn't believe him. *What does he mean by "feel the music"?* I wondered. *Did he literally mean feel the music? Like I can touch the notes or something?* I didn't understand. He would tell me to focus more deeply, and eventually I would feel the music. It was magical. I could feel the music's vibration penetrating into my skin, my pores, my soul, as if it was longing to become a part of me. As I'd play a piece, I could walk through a park on a spring day feeling blissful, or I could journey through a ravaging rainstorm of broken hearts and betrayal.

I could also trek through the cobblestone streets of Vienna and smell the aromas of rich coffee and freshly baked bread. Through the music I felt the pain and betrayal, and the heartache. I felt the breeze of spring. I could feel the innocent laughter of a child.

Mr. Stein made me feel this. He had an enormous effect on me, and his extraordinary talents, shown through in everything he taught me. I admired him immensely. You know, the less people speak about their greatness the more we think of it, and I thought about him a lot.

When I went to visit the old man, I had asked him about Victoria Brown. She was one of his old students and my best friend for many years. She was one of those rare people that you meet for the first time and feel like you've known forever. When we were sixteen, she moved with her family to California and I never saw her again. I asked Stein if he had heard from her, and he had said that he hadn't. Stein and I chatted more. It felt great to be around him. Somehow, he made every-thing seem right. It was comforting to see his stubby freckled hands again, and look into his thick pop-bottle glasses to see his pale blue eyes. He always made me see things differently and I loved him for that. We talked some about Victoria and some about the other goings-on in our lives. He was getting up there in years and had developed a slight cough and a constant raspiness in his voice. He would get out a monogrammed handkerchief and cover his mouth when he'd feel a tickle

THE CORE

coming on. I put my hand on his shoulder, and he'd looked at me with appreciation. I invited him to lunch.

We sat enjoying our lunch, casually chatting and reminiscing about the past. I had a patty melt with grilled onions and cheese. He eyeballed his overflowing sandwich—corned-beef on rye—taking large bites.

While we were sitting at the table, a tall, skinny waiter came over and asked, "Excuse me, are you Madison Phillips?" I was a little surprised that he knew my name. Slowly I said, "Yes, I'm Madison." Then he proceeded to tell me, "Someone near the bar says they know you."

Mr. Stein looked at me coyly and said, "Maybe it's Victoria." I looked at him and chuckled, "Yeah right." His pale blue eye winked at me.

I took a few bites from my sandwich, had a few sips of water, and then turned my head in the direction of the bar. At that moment, my stomach dropped twenty feet and my heart started palpitating like mad. I coughed and started sweating. I suddenly had a dry, pasty desert in my mouth. I looked at Mr. Stein as if I had just seen a ghost.

"Oh my God…it is." Mr. Stein looked up from his sandwich, surprised.

"It is what?" he asked.

"It's Victoria! She's walking right toward us." I could not believe that Stein and I had been talking about her all afternoon and then suddenly she appeared. She looked just how I remembered her. She sat down at our table and the three of us talked for hours. We caught up on everything. She told me that her father was transferred from California and that she and her family moved back to town a few weeks ago. She swung her auburn hair over her shoulder and paused. I knew she had something profound to say. I had a premonition.

"I'm going to Braxton College in the fall," she said.

As soon as I heard the word *Braxton*, I knew that was where I belonged. That was why I randomly met her that day—to reach the right decision and to go to Braxton. I believe the strangest coincidences happen when you're feeling restless or unsure about your direction in life and it is those coincidences that make your life flow into where you belong.

91

FIRST CLASS TICKET

It's funny the way things turn out. There have been times in my life where I've felt so lost, so confused, then something always happens to lead me in the right direction. Now, Victoria and I were as close as sisters.

After my beat writing class, I walked to the circle near the quad, where I saw Diana reading a large textbook. I walked over near her, but she didn't notice me.

"Diana?"

She looked up startled as if she wasn't expecting anyone to call her name. She popped her head up from her reading. I sat down next to her.

"Are you working on something?" I asked.

"I'm just reading this historical crap for my history class."

She continued reading where she left off, her eyes skimming from left to right. I glanced over at her khaki book bag on the bench that she must have purchased from an army surplus store. It was old and worn, full of buttons, pins, and iron-ons. It was covered with anarchy signs, a large iron-on of the Sex Pistols, and a button of a smiley face with a bullet to the forehead, plus another one that said "Stop Globalization."

To the right of her rebellious book bag, I noticed something that really caught my eye. It was a beautiful sketch of a three-dimensional landscape. The trees and brush jumped out at me off the paper and the elaborate elements of the branches and leaves were unbelievably detailed. There was a strong sense of movement in the work. The immensely intricate shading created an illusion that the leaves were blowing in the wind. It created a melancholy whispering among the trees and bushes that drew you in and begged for you to look deeper. It was full of insight and radiance. The landscape whispered something. *What was it whispering?* I thought for a moment. I looked at the movement in the leaves and branches again, the trees' somber pain was saying, "Listen." *Listen to me.* I studied the picture for a moment as Diana continued to read.

"Did you draw this?" I pointed to the picture. She looked up briefly and glanced at the picture.

"Yeah." She continued to read her large textbook, highlighting some passages in yellow. I gawked at the picture, completely in awe that she possessed the talent to draw such an amazingly involved landscape. I couldn't take my eyes off of it. It was breathtaking.

"I didn't know you were an artist, Diana."

"You never asked," she shrugged.

I looked at the picture again. "This is very good."

"Oh, it's horrible; the shading is all wrong. It's a disaster."

"I think it's beautiful."

"Yeah, well, it's not."

"I think you're wrong; it's unbelievable."

"Look, who told you you could look through my stuff?" she asked suddenly.

"Well, it was just sitting here, and I happened to notice it. It's really a great drawing. Are you an art major?"

"No."

"Why not? I think you have a lot of talent."

"Do you know anything about art?" she asked harshly.

"Yeah, I know a little bit, and I think this is really good."

"Well, that's not what my parents think—or anybody else for that matter." I could tell the words were like daggers to her heart as she said them with a low voice. Her tone cracked. Her shoulders turned inward.

"Are you enrolled in an art class here at school?" I inquired.

"No, my parents think it would be a waste of time and money." She didn't blink an eye.

"What? Don't they know how good you are?"

"No, and they don't care. They don't think studying art is a practical subject and they surely don't see it as a 'sensible career choice,' as my father says. He thinks it's just a hobby that's wasting my time."

"That's terrible," I replied. I looked at the drawing again. "How do you feel about your art work?"

"It's all I know," she said emotionally.

"So what are you going to do?" I wondered.

"Continue taking these stupid classes that don't mean shit to me and get a degree, so I can get a job I hate."

"You don't mean that."

"Yes, I do. I don't have a choice."

"What are you talking about? You have choices. You just have to make them into opportunities. Tell your parents how you feel, show them your work, tell them—"

She cut me off mid-sentence. "Look, I don't need another lecture, I just came from one. I'm fine."

"I think that later down the road, you'll be kicking yourself and wondering what could have been, and you'll really regret it."

"Well, that will be my problem, not yours."

I didn't say anything. All I could do was stare at the beautiful landscape she had created. *How could she let her talents pass her by and not utilize them?* Some people would give up their whole lives to have half the artistic ability she had. *I guess most of all, I'm upset with her parents for being so ignorant and close-minded. How could they stifle her abilities like that? Don't they want her to be happy?* I just didn't understand. There were a million other questions that I wanted to ask her, but I didn't want to offend her any more than I already had. I felt sorry for her again and guilty for prying.

Brian walked over to us. He looked cheery and full of life.

"Hey, girls."

Our vibe was negative and he could feel it. He immediately picked up on the mood we were in and the smile from his face slowly disappeared. "What's going on?"

"Not much," I said. But he knew I was being vague. I didn't want to add fuel to Diana's fire so I changed the subject.

"How are you, Brian? You're looking chipper."

"Why not? It's a beautiful day. I'm here with two beautiful girls. What's there not to be happy about?"

"Oh, you're very charming, Brian." I looked at him coyly.

"I thought so," he said,. His smile was electric, and I began to feel better. The conversation with Diana had brought my energy down and it was refreshing to be around Brian who was uplifting. He gazed at Diana's textbook, as her eyes were still glued to their boring, stupid pages.

"Whatcha reading there, Diana?"

"I have a quiz on the Ming Dynasty tomorrow for my Eastern history class and I need to learn this shit."

"Well if you think it's shit, why do you need to learn it?"

"I need to pass the quiz, don't I, smart ass?"

"Why?" he asked.

"What do you mean, why?" She was annoyed.

"If you don't care about what you're learning, why do you care if you pass the quiz?"

"I need to pass this class because it's one of my core classes. Without my core classes completed, I can't graduate."

"If you hate this class so much, why is it a part of your core classes? Shouldn't you enjoy what you're learning in your core classes? That is why they are building toward your major, toward your career. What do you eventually want to do, Diana?"

"My major is political science."

"I didn't ask you what your major was, I asked, what do you want to do with your life?"

"Become a lawyer," she said quickly.

"Is that what you want? Or is that what your parents want?" I asked.

"I don't know!" She yelled, slammed her textbook shut, and stood up abruptly. "I don't know. I'll figure it out." She spat the words at us.

"Want to know what I think?" Brian asked.

"No. Not really."

"Well, I'll tell you anyway. You need to master your core classes and graduate before you can move onto law school right?"

"Yeah, so what's your point?" Diana asked.

"My point is you'll never learn your core classes because you are failing to understand the core of yourself."

"Oh thanks, that's reassuring."

"He's right, Diana. When it comes to your life, you have to be the driver. Remember the dream you had? Your father was driving your car, and you wanted to avoid the rainstorm but the bridge to the other side was broken?"

"How do I fix the bridge? I don't know how. I don't know how to fix the frickin' bridge," she said in a desperate tone.

"I think I can tell you." We all turned toward the sound of a new voice in surprise. It belonged to a man of medium height and build, with wavy brown hair.

"I couldn't help overhearing your conversation. I thought this was an ideal time to chime in. I hope you don't mind." He smiled at us.

"No, no, go right ahead," I told him.

"I'm assuming that you're in Dr. Jacobs' class because I heard you analyzing a dream. So you know about the third eye, but you're not sure about which questions are the right questions to be asking. Is that right?"

"Yes, that's right." Diana said relieved.

"First of all you have to unravel the past to get to the core."

"What do you mean unravel? Like a banana?" I asked.

"Yeah." He chuckled. "Remember when you learned about ego traits and how you created your own ego because of the amount of energy your parents were giving you? And the lack of energy they gave you was because of their own ego trait?" The three of us nodded. "I hope you know which ego trait you possess and how to let it go. Do you feel as if you are letting it go?"

"Yes," we said to him.

"Good, because your core question is the only question you will have to ask from here on out. What is my purpose here? Since you already know and recognize your ego trait, you have to know and understand your parents' ego traits as well. Let's try to understand your current situation." He looked directly at Diana.

"What is your name?" He looked deep into her dark eyes.

"Diana," she mumbled.

"Okay, Diana, what is your ego trait?

"I guess I have the sympathy ego trait."

"Okay. What about your parents? What traits do they have?"

"My mom has a sympathy trait; and my dad has an intimidation trait."

"Are you sure he is an intimidator? Does he physically threaten you?"

"He is very intense and he's always in my face; he's very stubborn and he always takes everything so seriously like if I don't do something I'll suffer severe consequences. He makes me feel scared."

"Has he ever physically hurt you?"

"Well, he used to spank me when I was younger and ground me for not doing chores, or playing the radio too loud, that kind of thing. I was always terrified of him."

"But would he attack you for no good reason?"

"Well no, but it always had to be his way; there was never any other way."

"So his attitude scared you and threatened you, and you would cry and feel sorry for yourself all the time. And you would make him feel guilty for being so mean to you, right?"

"Yes."

"What about your mom? Would she make him feel guilty and sorry for her too?"

"My mom would always tell him how much she does for him and cry about how he's treating us. She tried to make him feel like a tyrant or something."

"Do you think that worked?"

"Sometimes he would try to do something nice for me, like he'd let me watch something on TV that wasn't educational. But he never said 'I'm sorry.'"

We all stared at Diana.

"What does your father do for a living?" he asked her.

"He's a coach."

"Ah, so he's an authority figure. What about your mom?"

"She's a housewife."

"So she's domestic and takes care of the house and your father and you? That's a very important profession. If your mother wasn't a housewife, what profession do you think she would have?"

"My mom is very creative, and she's very good with her hands. She can make anything. She made all the curtains in our house. She has a strong vision of creating something in her mind and then bringing it to life. She used to make all of my clothes when I was younger." The man looked at her clothes now. "She would still make me clothes if I continued to wear them but obviously, I don't." We looked at her overly large, baggy black shirt that read F***. I'm sure her mother didn't make that for her to wear. "She can create anything," Diana said proudly.

"Why do you think she never pursued her talents more?"

"Because my father wanted her at home with dinner ready, and the house clean, and the laundry done."

"So you think it's because she is scared of him? That is why she never pursued more for herself?"

"She's scared of disappointing him."

"Isn't that what you're doing?" The man looked at her sternly. "You're still letting him intimidate you. What did you say? He wants you to be a lawyer? This is very interesting. He wants you to be a lawyer because he wants you to be a reflection of himself, not of your mother. He wants you to be argumentative, and dominating, and manipulative, and an authoritarian. He views that profession as successful. He doesn't want you to be like your mother, creative and artistic. He views being creative as weak and subservient. He wants you to be strong like him."

"I think Diana is very strong," I said abruptly. "She's very opinionated and she's not afraid to tell it like it is. She has a very strong personality."

"The truth is the core of who you are is the synergy of the core of both of your parents. Therefore, you are a synergy of what your parents could not accomplish in their lifetime.

THE CORE

Truth #6—Your core is the essence of who you are. Your essence consists of the dreams your parents did not pursue. You are a synergy of both your parents' buried dreams. You must pursue your dreams to the fullest. If you bury your dreams, you bury gold.

"Your father wished he could communicate more effectively, but because he is so close-minded he knew that he could never make it as a lawyer and that's why he wants that for you. He only has the best intentions for you. He wants you to fulfill what he could not accomplish. And your mom just goes along with it because she doesn't want to disagree with him. So what you got from your parents is a strong personality from your father and a very artist creative side from your mother. It is that artistic side in you that you must pursue in order to fulfill your core question. Being an artist is who you are, so that you can move people with your creativity. Your strong personality will come out in your art, and the feeling in the work will be the heartbeat of the piece, making it salable. Your passion will show through in your art. You must create art work and you must use your strong personality in the work. Your core is to create art work that moves people."

"So that's what you think I should do?" Diana asked.

"Yes, because studying to be a lawyer won't make you happy, but your artwork will." Diana stared at the man for a moment as if she already knew that he was right. She just needed to here it from someone else. She needed validation.

"So what you're saying is in order to figure out our core question we need to figure out what each of our parents were trying to pursue with their life that they never accomplished and integrate those two attributes together and then we figure out who we are? Is that right?" Brian questioned.

"Yes, that is the key to determining your core question. Everyone has a purpose they are trying to fulfill, and every aspect of their life leads up to this purpose or helps shape this purpose. All of your in-

99

stincts, dreams, and insights are all based on the larger picture of your core question."

"Who am I?" Diana asked out loud. "I am an artist who moves people." She answered her own questions.

"Why is it a question?" I asked.

"It's a question because whenever you are uncertain about a situation or an event that is happening in your life, you must always target your smaller questions to your core question. But you must know your core question first. Once you establish your core question, everything will begin to make sense and your life will unravel in a more enlightening manner. That being said, what is your core question?" He was looking at me.

"My mother is a scrutinizer and so is my father. Therefore, I recognize that I have the indifferent ego trait. I was always asked so many questions, that I often felt like they were ridiculing or scrutinizing what I believed in," I explained. "My mother was a teacher, who later gave up her simple life to be in the social spotlight. She came from a humble upbringing, a small town in Connecticut with strong values and beliefs, but she longed for a more glamorous more fulfilling lifestyle. She married my father, an attorney, who came from a prestigious wealthy pedigree of attorneys and businessmen. His lifestyle fascinated my mother.

"My father is a very strong-willed man with a hardworking attitude. My mother is more a free spirit, and a lot more liberal in her beliefs about how the world should be. My father is very conservative and structured. He feels that he has to be busy all the time, often doing three things at once. My mother thinks that you should let the chips fall where they may and let it be. Because of the differences in their personalities, they argued a lot. They are no longer married, and they are much happier people now."

"So what was your mother's core question?"

"I don't know," I said.

"Well, what did she stand for but was never quiet able to achieve?"

"She loves children and she loves teaching children, and she always wanted to help the underprivileged by holding humanitarian events, by raising money from all of the socialites in the greater New York area. She wanted to do right for others but in a glamorous way. I know she got great gratification from helping the less fortunate, but it also came at a price. Most of the socialites at these events where in attendance to promote themselves by looking for other avenues to gain prosperity, whether politically or otherwise."

"So was your mother truly able to be a humanitarian and nurturer?"

"No, I guess she could never coordinate the two different aspects," I said.

"So she always wanted to be a humanitarian but in a social, sophisticated setting?"

"Yes, that's it," I said. "She's a humanitarian at heart, but because of the materialistic world, she thought her humanitarian side could never come through in a manner that suited her."

"What about your father?" he probed.

"Well, my dad believed that hard work paid off. He is a great attorney and has won many cases. He is very good at defending people and he is very articulate and intelligent. He sees both sides of the quarter and recognizes all possible circumstances. But it is his job to defend people, even if deep down in his heart he knows they committed crimes. It must be difficult to have to represent someone and argue a case for someone that he knows killed an innocent victim. Over the years, I think that has gotten him down, and I know he feels guilty about that. I see it in his gray hair and wrinkled face. Winning a case for a guilty man is the part of his job that has taken its toll on him, although he never talks about it."

"So where does that leave you?"

"I'm not sure," I said.

"Your mother is a nurturing, humanitarian with a materialistic side, and your father is an articulate communicator who is hindered by a lack of ethics in the system."

"I feel that I should be a journalist, but sometimes I'm not sure."

The man nodded and looked at me deeply. "That's a very interesting career path."

"Why do you say that?" I asked him.

"Think about it; your father is an ethical, articulate communicator who can't take his own advice, and your mother is a teacher and humanitarian who loves money. You see how both of your parents' core questions are contradicting themselves? You are here to make them straight. Through your writing and reporting, you can be the humanitarian with ethics. You will be writing and reporting about solid facts in a just and kind manner. You will be the communicator of people's stories, and because you will communicate their story as an ethical humanitarian, the public will read your work and you will have the ability to make a difference in your readers' lives.

"You are a journalist who can give the straight facts in a humanitarian and ethical manner. That is who you are. You are a journalist," he proclaimed.

I smiled from ear to ear. I was filled with immense gratification. I knew he was right, and I was thrilled to hear those words from him. I knew that my writing was very dear to my soul. I felt most alive when I wrote or made speeches, especially about controversial or critical subject matter. I was grateful to know that I was on the right path, even though I knew it all along. My eyes swelled and filled with tears of happiness. I was filled with love.

"What about you, guy? What's your core question?" he asked Brian.

We all looked at Brian, who was positively beaming during this conversation. I could sense he was gaining insight.

"I am a scrutinizer," he said. "That is my ego trait. I am working on letting go of it. However, I realize that I still need to ask questions of people to fully comprehend what is going on inside of them.

"Both of my parents have the indifferent drama. My father is an introverted man, who never showed his emotions. He's very cognitive and analytical because he is an electrical engineer. He is always building something, taking it apart, and then building it again. He is amazed by that. My mother is a nurse, she also fixes things, but instead of inanimate electrical objects she fixes people.

"What are both of your parents lacking?" the man asked.

"Well, my father is so in tune with fixing and critically thinking, he never takes the time to really communicate with the people who are important in his life. He has a wry personality and doesn't say very much; he just takes everything in and observes everything and rarely shares his thoughts with other people."

"My mother is always nurturing, but in a very erratic and out-of-control way. She talks a lot, is very outspoken, and is always on the run. She can never sit still and rationalize a situation before she goes running and jumping from one thing to another. My parents were there for me, but I often felt somewhat ignored by them."

"So knowing those things about your parents, where does that leave you?"

"Because my parents are fixers and healers, I know that I'm going into medicine. Throughout my life, I have always asked people questions and analyzed their answers because I am a scrutinizer. I am a synergy of both my parents, and I was always very curious about people and why they act the way that they do. Therefore; I'm going to study medicine of the psyche. I'm going to be a psychologist."

"You got it! That is who you are; you're a psychologist."

"Wow, Brian, that is great! You really figured out who you are from your parents. Good for you!" I smiled wide at him and he gave me a high five. All three of us were happy as if this newfound truth really touched us deep in the heart of our souls. I thought what a shame it was that people went through their entire lives and never realized who they were, or what they were doing here. It's all very simple when you recognize that you are an extension of what your parents were never able to accomplish in this life. Your children will be an extension of what you and your husband or wife never accomplished. This is a beautiful discovery.

Brian leaned over and hugged me, and I embraced him, feeling his love and giving him energy. I looked at him, and then noticed Diana standing off on her own. I motioned for her to join our hug. She was a little hesitant at first, but came near. All three of us had shared a group hug. It felt amazing. We held each other and squeezed each other feeling every positive ion in our bodies. We were glowing. Our faces smiled all over and we felt light and full of love. Brian looked over at the man, who gawked at us happily. We thanked him for helping us discover our core question.

"I wonder what will come next," I remarked. The man looked at all three of us as we still shared a hug.

"There is one thing that will make your core question come alive and without this you will not achieve your dream." We were still sharing a hug and feeling the energy of each other's bodies. I felt more alive than I'd ever felt before. We continued to hug, smiling and laughing.

"What is the one thing we need to make the dream happen?" I asked.

The man looked at us happily and said with a smile, "I think you already know."

After the hug, I looked down and saw a discarded apple core on the ground. I wanted to pick it up and savor the moment. I didn't pick up the apple's core, but I sure picked up my own.

Love gives itself; it is not bought.

—Henry Wadsworth Longfellow

IX

THE KEY OF LOVE

I woke up on Friday morning in love for the first time. Not with anyone in particular, just with the feeling. I hopped out of bed and started my day with a kick in my step and a song in my heart. I turned on the radio and the song that was blaring was "Friday I'm in Love" by the Cure. I started singing the words as I moved around the bathroom. Washing my face and brushing my teeth was a fun experience and not a chore this morning. I was so full of life I wanted to scream aloud. I felt my body tingle and I looked at my reflection and thought my face was beautiful. The fact that I was created from two microscopic living cells to make up this complex beautiful being that I was looking at in the mirror was extraordinary for me to think about. The loud music woke up Victoria as I heard her closet door slam. *I know she's crabby in the morning, but I can change all that.*

I walked into the kitchen and toasted a bagel, got Victoria's cereal and milk, and sat down at the kitchen table. A fashion magazine was strewn across the table, with a model looking as airbrushed as ever on the cover. I noticed that we are living in a society that places great value on the exterior of the core. The one thing in our culture that matters is the meat around the core. That made me upset. I now realize that all we needed was the core, because without the core there was no exterior. I noticed the feature article read "Top five reasons to love." Top five? Why are there so many? It must be simpler than that? There is only one reason to love and it a glorious reason. The music continued to blare out of the radio as I bobbed my head to the beat and ate my bagel with cream cheese.

Victoria came out of the bathroom with tired eyes and poured her cereal in the bowl. I sang the words to the song under my breath.

"You're very happy this morning," she commented. "Oh wait, did someone spend the night?" She walked into my bedroom and took a look at my bed.

"Nope, nobody's there," I said.

"Oh, I thought maybe you got lucky last night with that baseball player."

" Jeff?" I asked. "No way, I'm just happy. Do I have to get laid to be happy?"

"No, but it helps." Victoria said matter-of-factly.

We both looked at each other and started to laugh. She was always making some kind of perverted comment and I found it intriguing. The giggling slowly subsided.

"So what's going on?"

"I'm just happy; this philosophy class is really turning out to be a great experience."

"So what truth did you learn yesterday?"

"We learned about our core question and how this question is your purpose in life, and that everything that happens to you is in correlation with your core question."

"Wow, you're really eating this stuff up, huh?" Victoria asked.

"Yeah, I think it's really cool. I wish you could have experienced it with me."

"Hmm....Maybe I'll take that class next semester; who teaches it?"

"Dr. Jacobs. Oh—I wanted to ask you. Do you want to go to the baseball game on Sunday?"

"With the Plague?"

"It could be really fun, and we don't have to be around her the whole time."

"I don't know. I might go with John to the country."

"Who's John? The one from Syracuse?"

"No, that was Jared."

106

"John is from Rhode Island," she said, as if I should know these things.

"Oh…well, ask him to come along."

"I don't know, Madison."

She slurped her cereal and chewed loudly, while looking at the magazine on the table.

"Do you like this guy?" I asked her.

"He's all right, I guess; we're just having fun."

"Oh really? How much fun?" We laughed again and she picked up on my sarcasm.

"As much fun as he's able to perform." She winked at me and I started cracking up.

"Freud ain't got nothing on you," I told her, laughing. She giggled loudly as the radio kept singing.

After my English class on romantic literature let out, I headed over to Brian's apartment, where he had suggested we meet at two o'clock. I was a little leery about going over to his place. Part of me really wanted to see Jeff and another part of me wanted to forget that I ever met him. Diana had stated that her dad would freak out if he discovered she was at one of his player's apartments. He was always pissy about that kind of thing. Brian reassured her that nobody would be around at that time. He wanted to grill hamburgers and brats and sit on his deck. It sounded kosher to me so that's where we decided to meet.

His apartment was filled with movie posters of the *Godfather, Scarface,* and Robert DeNiro. There were different beer bottles from brews around the world on top of the end table behind the couch. Two Sony PlayStations were scattered on the floor near the oversized television. The apartment was pretty clean, but it still smelled like boys. I pictured Jeff lounging on these couches in his sweatpants and messy hair watching television and drinking beers while scratching the occasional itch. I created a sexy visual in my head. I noticed a girly magazine on the coffee table and looked to see who it was addressed to but couldn't make out the name without lifting it up. I didn't want to be too nosy, so I walked away from it.

FIRST CLASS TICKET

We went to the back of the apartment onto the sunny wooden deck that overlooked a lawn full of weeds and dandelions. The crabgrass was thick and mangy like an unkempt overgrown beard. There was charcoal in bags up against the house and white plastic furniture sticky from beer. An empty pony keg sat used in the corner of the deck. The high afternoon sun scorched my face.

"There's shade over on this side," Brian said, trying to be hospitable. He pointed to a large weeping willow tree that shaded the east side of the deck. He then began to fuss with the grill, rustling with the heavy bags of charcoal, and cleaning last night's dinner off with the brush.

"Let's get this baby going." As he ignited a high flame, it made a loud *whoosh*…and its orange fury erupted like a volcano.

"Shit, damn near burned my eyebrows off!" Brian exclaimed, as Diana laughed loudly.

"You think that's funny, Diana, huh?" She laughed aloud at his antics.

He grilled the bratwurst and hamburgers, throwing American cheese on the burgers, one by one. Diana was enjoying her cigarette, as I tried to set the sticky plastic table with paper plates. The wind was blowing them off the table so I put a two-liter Coke bottle on top of them to keep the paper plates from flying off.

We ate our hamburgers and brats in the shade of the weeping willow, while talking and laughing. We were all in a great mood and it was nice hanging out with them. I felt close to them as if they were really my friends and I enjoyed their company.

"That was probably the best cheeseburger I ever ate," I said.

"Thanks, Brian," Diana said, with a full mouth.

"Anytime, girls. Anytime." He took a few swigs of Coke. "You know, I also moonlight as a chef."

"Really?" I asked.

"Yeah, I cook all these guys dinner."

"What a nice roommate you are."

108

I wanted to ask Brian about Jeff, but I didn't want him to wonder why I was asking.

"Isn't it great that we know our core question?" I asked instead.

"Yeah, and the funny thing is all three of us knew it all along, but were looking for validation."

"I've decided that next semester I am changing my major to art," Diana said, "and I don't care what my parents want from me anymore. I'm going to do what makes me happy."

"That's great, Diana." Brian and I smiled at her. I was so happy she came to that realization. She looked like a weight had been lifted off her shoulders.

"That man last night said we already know what the missing link is that we need to answer our core question."

"What do you think the missing link is?" Diana asked.

"I have an instinct but I don't want to say it just yet." I looked at her.

"Fine, be that way, Madison." I could tell she was kidding. I was happy that she could laugh about it. While talking with Diana, a strong gust of wind blew through our hair and nearly blew me over. The paper plates from the table flew off and scattered everywhere on the deck.

Then, I heard the doorbell ring inside the apartment. Brian quickly picked up the paper plates and excused himself to go inside to see who was at the door. I thought maybe it was Jeff, but of course he wouldn't have rung the doorbell to his own place. But maybe he forgot his key. My heart was in my throat. I had a premonition that whoever was at the door was somehow important. I had a few sips of Diet Coke and Diana lit up another cigarette. We waited for Brian to return, and through the screen door I could hear him talking loudly to another man inside.

The screen door swung open as Brian and a tall, rugged-looking man with wild eyes walked onto the deck. Brian was smiling all over, and I could tell he was very happy and excited to see his friend.

"Girls, let me introduce you to my buddy. This is Nathan. Nate was studying abroad in Spain and he just came back. Nathan, this is Diana and Madison." He shook both of our hands with a warm smile, and sat down beside us at the sticky table, crossed his leg onto his knee, and looked up at my face. He was tan, almost wind-burned, and his hazel eyes twinkled in the bright sunshine. His dark eyebrows were bushy and untamed, as his long black eyelashes outlined his big eyes. I was instantly drawn to his mystery.

"So what part of Spain were you in?" I asked, trying to break the ice.

"I was in Barcelona. I had a beautiful, remarkable experience there." He looked right through me. He was very articulate and polite and spoke with confidence and poise.

"In fact, I could have stayed there another year, but it was my time to come home."

"How did you know it was your time to come back?" Brian asked him.

"Because I experienced what I needed to learn in Spain and it was time to come home and be able to experience what I learned there, here. I made so many extraordinary discoveries, some nights I would sleep outside in the plaza and be awakened by the most beautiful sun behind the whitewashed houses. I walked through the narrow streets, saw the most gorgeous churches, and traveled through the most surreal fields. I met friendly, hospitable people that welcomed me into their homes and their vineyards."

"What about the clubs and nightlife? Didn't you party a lot?" Brian asked him.

"I went out every night at first, but I didn't think that was the most rewarding way to experience my time there. I wanted to really get to the 'core' of what Spain was about, and I couldn't do that simply by being in crowded dance clubs struggling to make conversations over pounding music."

"It's funny that you used the word 'core.' Do you think you discovered the 'core' of Spain?" I asked him.

"Yes, Madison." He looked right through me again and inched closer to me. "Not only did I discover the 'core' of Spain, but I discovered the core of myself." As soon as he said that, chills ran through my body. *Another coincidence*, I thought. *Who was this guy?* I couldn't take my eyes off him. The way he spoke, the way he looked, he was regal. Regal in

110

every sense of his being. He was wise, worldly, and full of peace. I was amazed.

"Dude, we just found our core question yesterday, during our philosophy experiment," Brian interjected. "It was awesome! We learned that we are a synergy of both of our parents' cores, and we are here to accomplish what they could not fulfill in their lifetime." I felt myself becoming lighter, more aware, more in tune. Diana was also listening intensely.

"That's really great! So the three of you are experiment partners?" We looked at him and nodded.

He smiled at us and went on. "I went to Spain to experience a new culture and discover how they lived, what was important to them, what they stood for, and what they valued. It seems that in the States, people are so wrapped up in the monotony of life and the meaningless aspects of their jobs. Most people are stuck in the same routine for twenty years, too afraid to try something new, to venture out and find what makes them happy, because after so much time in monotony, they lost what their happiness is. Once you ignore your core for long periods of time, you soon forget about it and it sinks deeper and deeper inside, therefore making it almost impossible to come out. Most people's dreams are so deeply embedded because over time, people become so infested with the negativities of life and the prejudices of the world, that they think their dreams are unattainable. I saw happiness in the people of Barcelona and it was because they know something that we do not."

"What did you discover from them?" I wondered.

"That was the thing, I thought that the discovery would be complex and take a long time to figure out, but in fact it was the most basic principle of all. I discovered that the only thing people in the world need to survive is love. Once you discover your core, you must fulfill your core question with love. Love is the only thing that will bring your core into life. Without love you cannot fully achieve your dreams."

"Do you mean the love of others? Or your love for someone else?" I asked the handsome stranger, and he looked at me kindly.

FIRST CLASS TICKET

"No, I mean the love you possess inside. It's the feeling that you get when you're enthused about something, or inspired, or elated about the opportunities in the future. If you don't recognize the love of the universe, and what it is trying to tell you with coincidences, then it will take you longer to fulfill your core and you might never reach it. You cannot achieve your core blindly. You must be open to the love of the universe that is already inside you and be able to recognize that it's there helping you all the while."

"How did you find your core?" Diana asked him.

"It's a long story. Is it ever a short one?" he asked with a chuckle. "My first day in Spain was a nightmare. I arrived in the marketplace with my suitcase and I was trying to find where the house was that I was staying at. I asked many people of the address and the family name, but nobody knew where it was or who the family was. I got in a cab and I asked the cabdriver to take me to the address I had. He took me for a long ride through the city and then discovered he had no idea where it was. I had already paid him forty dollars, and he dropped me off at a coffeehouse on the west side of town. I was lost, I had no idea where I was going, and I was out forty bucks.

"I went into the coffeehouse and asked the bartender if he knew where this address was. He said he couldn't understand me. My Spanish was good, but he could tell I was American. I tried asking him again, but nothing. Then I pointed to the address on my paper and he just shook his head. My luggage stood at a table five feet away from me. Frustrated with the man, I put the written address in my pocket and turned to get my luggage. My luggage was gone. Someone had walked off with it. I thought the bartender was trying to distract me so that his friend could steal my luggage. When I confronted the bartender he acted like he didn't know what I was talking about. He said he hadn't seen a suitcase. There I was, lost, in a strange country, no luggage, and out forty dollars. Thank God I still had money on me. I thought about taking the next flight back to the States. I was so discouraged, so heartbroken, so depressed. I thought that coming to Spain had been a terrible mistake."

112

"So what did you do?" I asked him, on the edge of my seat.

"I walked out of the coffeehouse to a nearby church. The church was very old, and I sat down on its front doorstep. I put my head in my lap; I was almost in tears. I prayed to God to help me and send me a sign of where to go next. I sat there for an hour, but no sign. As I sat on the church steps completely depressed, I suddenly saw a vision of myself walking up a steep hill. I couldn't see the destination, but in my vision I was making progress. I saw the nearby hill with houses at the top and I decided to take the climb. It was late afternoon and I was sweating in the dry heat. I kept trudging up the hill. It was so steep that I felt blisters forming on my feet. On my way up the hill, I passed a man walking the other way. I pulled out my paper with the address. I showed the man the address on the paper. My Spanish was good, but he could tell I was American. He said, 'I'll tell you where that house is for twenty dollars.'

"'You can't charge me for directions!' I yelled at the man.

"'I'm not lost,' he said, 'you are.' I couldn't believe it, from the moment I got into Barcelona, everything bad that could have happened did. I was hesitant to give the man the money because I didn't trust him. He might not even tell me the right house anyway. I had been duped by a cabdriver, my luggage was stolen, I was lost, and I had blisters the size of quarters on my feet. I thought for a moment that I might have written down the wrong address, but it had to be right.

"It was siesta time, and I knew there would be no one on the streets for another two hours. This man was my only hope. I gave him the twenty dollars, and he asked for the address. When he looked at the address, his face grew blank. He checked the address again and then looked at my face. He patted me on the shoulder. 'C'mon I'll walk you to the house, I know where it is,' he said. Relieved, I smiled, and I walked up the hill with him, my blisters killing me the whole way up.

"We arrived at the top of the hill at a white stucco house with Spanish-tile roof. There was a large courtyard in the middle of the house and a statue water fountain near the front door. I became a little nervous about meeting the family that I was to live with for three months. I thanked the man for showing me the way, and I shook his hand kindly. He shook my hand in return and gave me a bright smile. At that point, I was expecting him to walk away, but he kept smiling at me. We stood near the doorway as my palms grew sweaty. I thought maybe he wanted a tip or something. I reached into my pocket to grab a few more dollars. He patted me on the back and said, 'No, no, no.' I didn't understand what he wanted from me. He then reached down into his pocket, pulled out some keys, and unlocked the front door. I was shocked. I didn't know what to do. 'This is my house.' he said. 'Come inside.' I couldn't believe it. I was tempted to run out, but I went inside anyway. I walked into a quaint living room. The aroma, of spicy food filled the house. The Spanish furniture was tasteful and I noticed a beautiful wood-burning fireplace in the corner. It was a nice home. But I was still very confused about this man, and he could sense it on my face.

"'I knew you were the boy that was staying with us,' he said in broken English.

"'So why didn't you say anything when we first met on the road up the hill?'

"'Because I wanted to learn about you, about your character. I don't let just anyone stay with me and my family.'

"'Then why did you charge me for directions to the house?'

"'Because if you want something very bad, you must pay for it. You wanted to find the house, right? And you came to Spain to learn something right? Well, you paid twenty dollars for this learning experience so far, and that is all I will ever ask of you.'

"'Since I arrived here, I've already paid 40 dollars for a cab ride to nowhere, my luggage was stolen. I had everything in that suitcase, now I have nothing.' I was so upset and frustrated, and now this. I didn't understand this man, and I didn't think I could live with someone I didn't trust.

"'You have everything,' the man said to me.

"'How do I have everything?'

"'Come over here.' He waved his hand toward his body, motioning to follow him. He took me to the closet near the front door. As he

THE KEY OF LOVE

opened the closet, my eyes opened wide. There was my suitcase, with forty dollars on top of it. My mouth dropped. This was really getting weird.

"How did my suitcase end up in his closet? And where did the forty dollars come from? I was really angry with the man. 'You had the cabdriver take me to nowhere, and you stole my suitcase? Who are you? What kind of game are you playing?' I was fuming. The man put his hand on my shoulder to calm me down. He looked sincerely into my eyes.

"'It was not a game, it was a test.'

"'So you stole my money and my suitcase to test me? Why? I don't understand.'

"'I wanted to see how you would react to a stressful situation, what would you do, how would you get by? I wanted to know if you had a good character. If I didn't like your reaction, I would not invite you to live with me and my family.'

"'So did I pass your test?' I asked him sarcastically.

"'After I had my friend at the coffeehouse take your suitcase, I walked by and saw you sitting on the steps of the old church. Your head was down and you were praying. You looked sad and humble, and at that point I knew you where a good person and a trustworthy person. In a large city like Barcelona there are so many things that you could have done. You could have beat up the cabdriver and the bartender. You could have gone to a bar and gotten drunk to forget your problems; you could have found a brothel to fix your problem. You could have done anything, but you went to a church and prayed. That was why I helped you find my house, because you have a good character. When you got to the church, how you did feel?' he asked me.

"'I felt terrible, I felt helpless. I was lost, and I had lost my suitcase. I was thinking about going back home actually.'

"'Then when you started to pray how did you feel?'

"'I felt better, I had more energy and more strength but I still didn't receive the answer I wanted.'

"'What did you receive, instead?'

"'I received a vision of walking up a hill in an unknown direction, but I felt that I was making progress.'

"'What feelings were you having when you saw your vision?' he asked.

"'I was feeling better,' I said.

"'You were feeling inspired and grateful that you had a vision, otherwise you never would have listened to your vision, and you never would have started to climb the hill.'

"'Yeah, you're right. I told him. I think I was feeling something from within to make me follow my vision.'

"'What was that something?'

"'I'm not sure, I don't know.'

"He looked me dead in the eye. 'It was love. The feeling that helped you follow your vision was love.' He looked at me sincerely, and he was full of light. Here this man was, a total stranger, and he was telling me about love in a way that I never thought of before.

"I thought for a moment, and then looked at him. 'On my way up the hill, why did you test me again, if you knew I was a good person?'

"'I tested you at that crucial point to see how much you wanted your vision to come true. I wanted to know how much you believed in your vision. A lot of people receive visions, and they act upon them, but it takes a special person to completely make that vision a reality. At that point, you could have told me to get lost, but instead you paid me the money, and I showed you the way. You must have wanted it bad enough to do whatever it took to find my house. You still had faith.'

"I thought about that for a long moment. He said, 'Your journey here will be a constant uphill battle, but if you feel love, you will make great progress. That is the only way you will learn, and experience what you came to experience here in Spain.' He patted me on the shoulder again, gave me my twenty dollars back, and said, 'Dinner is ready.'"

We were staring at Nathan in amazement. "Did that really happen?" Diana asked.

"Yes, that was exactly the way it happened. From that point on, me and the man and his family were great friends and he taught me many things."

"How does this help your core?" Brian asked his friend.

Truth #7—*You must use the love of the universe to make your core come true. The love you possess inside is also the love of the universe. Use your love to make your dreams a reality. Once you realize your dream, the entire universe conspires to help you achieve it. This is the key of love.*

"I've always had a feeling that I wanted to travel and explore the cultures of the world. I was always very fascinated with people, and my experience in Spain validated to me that my quest for travel and cultures is what I should be doing. That is why I am studying sociology. In fact, because of that experience, I am so excited to learn about my sociology major and to pursue my dream of becoming a doctor of sociology. All the homework and papers and tests now seem so worthwhile to me. I happily study for them and write my papers with love. Without the love for what I am doing, there is no point even to perform it. I must feel the love for what I am learning, to reach my short-terms goals, and my short-term goals will enable me to reach my long-term goals."

"That is so true," I said to him, as he looked back at me with wonder. I was amazed by his wisdom and his love. He was a young man, but his knowledge was light-years beyond his time. He was projecting his love upon us, and I could sense it in my heart.

"What about other emotions? How do you feel them?" Diana inquired.

"Well, the man in Spain taught me that you must fully feel the emotions you are having. You have to really allow yourself to feel the love, or pain, or joy, or sorrow. You have to let them into your soul and experience them and don't suppress them because those feelings will live inside you until you are ready to feel them, and at that point they will erupt into ugliness. All the negative thoughts and feelings you had will come out at once, and you will be out of balance and out of control."

"So if you become so sad that you feel like crying, you should cry?" Brian looked at him, trying to be macho.

"Yeah, man. If you become so moved that you feel like crying you have to cry. You must allow yourself to feel that sadness. Once you fully feel that emotion, you can then let it go and move on. I know, it is not culturally acceptable for a man to openly cry," he admitted, "but one should not buy into societal norms when you are feeling an emotion. Suppressing that emotion will build inside you, and you will be carrying it around with you like baggage. The soul longs to be free, it should not be walking with chains around it. By suppressing emotions you chain your soul down. Hence, people become depressed and draw away from their core. You must recognize that emotions are the way the soul lets you know it's there, and it's a beautiful discovery to feel your emotions fully, disconnect from them, and then let them go."

"What do you mean 'disconnect'?" I asked him.

"Once you fully experience an emotion, you must admit that you experienced it, and then detach your soul from it. It takes time to disconnect from the pain or sorrow. That is the healing process. Feeling pain is like a wound, it takes time to heal, but if it heals right, there won't be a scar. When time allows you to disconnect, the wound heals and then you are ready to move on."

"I don't get it," Brian said. He was looking at his friend as if he was talking a foreign language.

"Let me give you an example. Remember being little and falling off your bike and scraping your knee? Remember how you felt? What happened? You felt the pain, and cried—cried openly. You felt the stinging, and the soreness through your whole body, and you cried loudly. Your mom washed off the wound and put a healing ointment on it. As she did that, the wound burned more, the pain was even more intense, almost unbearable, and you wailed even louder. She then put a bandage on the wound, dried your eyes, and sent you on your way. After a few hours of cartoon watching, and six Oreo cookies later, you forgot about your knee and were outside riding your bike again later that day. You see how that worked? As a child we subconsciously recognize that our bodies and souls need to feel the emotion, take time to heal, disconnect from the pain, and then let it go. This is because children are closer to their souls, than adults are, because they are so innocent. Adults are too afflicted by the negativities of the world to be that close to their soul. But there is a way one can be close to their soul all the time, and that's by feeling emotions and feeling the love of the universe. The love of the universe is also your own love."

"What?" Brian asked.

"I'll get into that later."

"Is this only true when dealing with pain?" Diana asked him.

"It's true for all emotions, especially for times of pain."

"But we should be able to feel love all the time?" I asked him looking into his hazel eyes.

"Yes, Madison, for the most part you should be able to always feel love, especially when you are going through a healing process, because it will help you overcome the pain."

"I still don't get how you could feel love all the time. That seems weird." Diana looked at him puzzled.

"Don't worry, you'll learn," he reassured her.

The wind was blowing briskly. It blew the leaves in the trees, causing them to sway. I felt a sense of euphoria. I felt one with the wind as well, for it was the wind that blew him into our circle, and I didn't want him to leave.

"What are the three of you doing tomorrow?" he asked us with a smile. We all looked at him.

"I am going to the beach in the morning; why don't you all join me?"

"Great, we will be there, buddy," Brian said, as we all smiled at Nathan. He was beautiful and enlightening. I was full of love. The four of us sat there in the afternoon sun as the wind blew us closer together. Brian switched on the small radio that was outside and a song rang out loudly.

We were created from the dirt of the Earth;
we are the Earth, as the Earth is us.

—Anonymous

X

BODY OF EARTH

The distance from my apartment to the beach was almost a mile. I decided to walk instead of taking my old hand-me-down silver Volvo. I called it the "mom car."

It was eight o'clock in the morning and I felt that I was really changing. I never got out of bed before ten on Saturday mornings unless I absolutely had to, but this morning I woke up willfully. I thought about how absolutely interesting the first week of the semester had become and how refreshing our strange philosophical trip had been. I reflected on how I had an instinct I would see a familiar face on the first day of class and I ran into the Plague. I thought it was a jinx at first, but now I was beginning to think it was a blessing in disguise.

I was so impressed with Nathan, but I feared never seeing him again. When he invited us to the beach, I wanted to jump out of my seat and praise God. The funny thing is, I know he didn't invite us to the beach simply to see Diana and me in our bikinis; he had another agenda, a higher purpose. I really liked that about him. Here I was complaining about vacant, shallow people at this college, but the truth was, if you put yourself into different circles, you will find more interesting people who are on your wavelength. You just have to get through the awkwardness and fear of being around different people, but after you let your guard down, and they let down theirs, good things happen. You find more similarities than differences. You even discover yourself.

I wondered why Nathan wanted to meet at the beach of all places. I actually liked the idea, and I smiled to myself, admiring the old Victo-

120

rian row houses on the street. The wind swept through my white cotton blouse. I galloped down the street whistling the entire way. I could hear the surf pounding hard against the sand as the seagulls and pigeons chirped obnoxiously. The wind was carrying them away. They fluttered their wings trying to stay on course, but the wind was too strong. It was forcing them to take another path and move in a new direction. They chirped loudly in retaliation.

I arrived at the beach to find Diana writing something in the sand with her foot. She was dragging her heal and pushing the sand into formations that created large letters in the brown dust. I walked closer to her to try to make out what the words were saying. At first, I thought she was writing profanities. I squinted my eyes and walked closer. The misty, humid air was salty on my lips as the wind sifted through the sand.

"What does that say, Diana?" I asked, still squinting my eyes to read the letters in the sand.

"Read it, aloud," she said.

I tried to make out the letters. "Keystone, True, and Jeremiah. What is that?"

"I don't know what the hell it is," she said. "But for the past two days, I've been thinking this phrase. I can't get it out of my head."

"Have you ever heard it before? Is it something from television? Did you read it in a book?" I asked her.

"No, I have no idea who it is, what it is, or what it means," she said. "But I had to say it or write it out somewhere because it's been driving me nuts. I've been going mad."

"Whatever it is it sounds funny. Keystone, True, and Jeremiah. Keystone, True, and Jeremiah. Keystone, True, and Jeremiah." We kept repeating those words and laughing to ourselves. We started making a little dance to the rhythm of the words. We were laughing, as Brian and Nathan walked up to us. Even the guys joined in and had a good laugh. Keystone, True, and Jeremiah too. Mocking us they began singing the rhythm of the words. It became a cheer of sorts and we all laughed. Keystone, True, and Jeremiah too. We cheered loudly, dancing, laughing, and clanking our hips together. We must have looked like such dorks, like complete idiots, but we didn't care. We danced and sang in triumph, as if we'd just conquered the world. Keystone, True, and Jeremiah too. Keystone, True, and Jeremiah too.

"What the hell is 'Keystone, True, and Jeremiah too'?" Brian asked finally.

"We have no idea," Diana said. "It's just a phrase that has been stuck in my mind for two days. I finally let it out."

"Well, good for you, Diana!" Nathan said with a huge smile, and we all laughed.

Brian and Nathan spread out beach towels on the sand and set up a cooler with drinks alongside of us. The wind was strong, and the sky was slightly overcast as the sun was trying to peek through the gray clouds. One of the beach towels was a Hawaiian girl in a bikini with a pink lei around her neck. It must have been Brian's towel, and Diana quickly sat on it. For a while, we looked out at the ocean and watched the tide roll in. The waves were high and they crashed wildly onto the sand. Brian found a large seashell and put it to his ear. He was listening intently to hear the ocean inside the seashell.

"I can hear it!" Brian shouted. "I can hear the ocean inside this shell."

"You're not hearing the ocean in the shell; you're just imagining that it's actually inside of it," Diana said to him.

"No, I can really hear it—the wind and the pounding surf. Why do you think that is?" he asked Nathan.

"You can hear the ocean inside the shell, because that shell was created from the ocean." Brian stared at the shell, following its contours, lines, and ridges, which were once individual sand particles that formed together to make up one solid entity. He examined the lines and ridges of the shell that were formed by the salt water of the ocean. The high and low tides washed over the sand a billion times to create the lines and contours of the shell. The shell was a product of the ocean. And the ocean was a product of the shell.

"You can hear the ocean in the shell, because the shell is, in fact, the ocean," Nathan declared.

"How so?" Diana asked.

"All the particles and matter that make up this shell were once the sand particles of the ocean that formed together over time to construct the attributes of the shell. With the tides of the ocean and the elements of salt, oxygen, and water, they produced one solid mass."

"That's amazing." Brian looked at the shell with appreciation. "I never really thought of that before; one can hear the ocean in the shell, because the shell is actually the ocean."

"They are one together," I said with enthusiasm. "The core of the shell is the ocean and the ocean's core is the shell."

"That's right, Madison. Isn't that cool?" Nathan asked me. We stared at the large white shell with its flecks of brown and gray intertwined in the contours of its edges, folds, and rims. It was a beautiful shell and we were amazed by its old magnificence. In the distance, the horizon seemed an infinity away. We noticed tiny white boats bobbing in the waves of the ocean's splendor. We all enjoyed the scenery for a moment, taking deep breathes of the salty air that was sticking to our skin. The humidity was curling my hair as I could feel it moistness penetrate my once straight hair into curly locks.

Brian and Nathan were still marveling about the shell and smiling widely at the landscape. We stared at the ocean, as the waves curled over and washed the sand from the shore deeper into the heart of the ocean. The ocean was recycling itself from moment to moment with every wave. For the ocean was never the same place twice, changing every moment and renewing itself into a more efficient existence. The ocean has its own mind, its own heartbeat, and its own soul. It knows exactly what to do at any given instant. It's pure synchronicity.

"How is that possible?" I asked.

"How is what possible?" Brian looked at me still marveling at the shell.

"How does the ocean know what to do? How does it know to have a high tide or a low tide, or to be wavy or calm? How is that possible?" I asked.

Nathan looked at me and grinned widely. "How does your body know what to do without you telling it? You never tell your body, now it's time to digest my food, or now it's time to grow my hair, or now it's time for my heart to beat faster. Or now it's time for my pancreas to create insulin. It just does it."

"So what are you saying? The ocean is like our body?" I asked.

"Yes, it's a part of your body. What is your body primarily made of?"

"Water," I said.

"Right. How did it get there?"

"I drank it?"

"That's true you drink water, but all of the cells in your body need water to develop, to live, and then to rejuvenate themselves and grow new cells."

"I don't understand, I'm not sure what you mean."

"Visualize the earth in your mind. What do you see?"

"I see a solid, round mass with large parts of blue water and large parts of brown land."

"That's from a distance," he pointed out. "Now visualize the earth at a closer glance. What do you see?"

"I see blue sky, green grass, brown dirt, green trees, oceans, rivers, lakes, tributaries, rocks, mountains, hills, and land."

"Okay, now describe your body." Nathan said.

"Describe my body? Is this a trick question?" I asked, trying to be funny.

"No, there is no perversion here," he laughed. "I promise. Now go ahead." I looked at him coyly for a second then proceeded to tell him.

"Well, it's made up of many bones that make up a skeleton, veins, muscles, a heart, lungs, a liver, and so forth, that is all covered with skin.

"Okay, now look at that tree over there." Nathan was energized as he pointed to a tall tree that was blowing in the wind behind where we were sitting. "If that tree were a body part, what would it be? Concentrate on the functions of the tree and what the tree represents to the universe at large."

I thought about it, looking at the tree for a long moment. "I know that trees need carbon dioxide to breathe, and they give off oxygen, which is the opposite of what a human needs to survive. Humans need oxygen to breathe, and we give off carbon dioxide. We breathe in what they exhaust and they breathe in what we exhaust."

Nathan looked at me hard. "Good, now isn't it true that trees give us exactly what we need to survive and we as humans do the same for the trees and other living plants in the world?"

"Yes, that's true, so the trees and plants are the lungs of the universe?"

"That's right, Madison. Without our lungs we cannot breathe; that is why trees are so important to the universe, because they give us the air to breathe.

"The land is the skin and bone of our body. This solid ground of rock and soil, forms the solid structure of our body, as they form the solid structures of the earth. The rivers, lakes, and tributaries are the blood in the body, pumping blood and nutrients to our vital organs in our body. As these bodies of water distribute nutrients to the soil, they create proteins that can be consumed into the body of the earth. We have discovered the trees are the lungs, the rivers are the veins, and the land is the skin and bones."

I thought about this for a moment. Then a new thought came to me. "What about the heart? What is the heart of the universe?" I asked him, intrigued by the direction the conversation was headed.

"You tell me," he said. I thought about it as I looked at him. I honestly had no idea. I had never thought how the earth is relevant to the body. It seemed like a really strange concept. "What does the heart symbolize in the body? What is its function?" he asked me.

"Well, the heart pumps blood through the entire body, and then recycles the blood," I said hesitantly.

"So what is the blood of the universe?"

"The oceans, lakes, rivers, and tributaries?"

"That's right. What do these bodies of water need to survive, to be recycled through the atmosphere?" I had no answer. "I'll give you a clue: Think of it as a meteorologist would. What do you know about the science of the universe that helps recycle water through the earth?"

I thought longer and harder. "Mmm…" I hesitated.

"It's trying to peek through the clouds right now," he said.

"The sun!" I answered excitedly.

"That's right. The sun is the heart of the universe. The heat of the sun is able to evaporate water from the oceans and lakes and rivers and recycle it throughout the land giving those ecosystems water, nutrients, and the proteins necessary to live. The heart of the human body is just like the sun. The sun is the energy source and the life source of the universe. Without the sun, the earth would not be able to function properly. This is also true in the human body; without the heart pumping and recycling blood throughout the body, the body would shut down. That is why the heart is constantly beating, because this is a constant process, which is also true of the weather. There is always a weather system in the world that is happening at all times."

"The heart is the sun," I said again. It completely made sense to me, although it was something I never took the time to realize on my own.

"So if the heart is the sun, the lungs are the trees, the veins are the oceans, lakes, and tributaries, the skin and bone is the land, then what is the brain?" I wondered.

"The brain is the most complex of all," said Nathan. "The brain encompasses everything."

"What do you mean?" I asked.

"Why do you think that we only use ten percent of our brain power?" He looked deep into my eyes.

"I don't know, probably because we have not progressed enough as humans to use more of it," I said.

"Yes, that's right Madison, but it goes much deeper than that. The brain that we have possesses the entire energy of the universe. Our brains are infinite, as the universe is infinite."

"So what you're saying is that the brain is the universe at large?"

"The brain is the universe, with all of its energy, knowledge, and infinite wisdom."

"The brain is the entire universe?" It was very bizarre to realize that within us is the entire universe. I thought for a moment as Nathan projected a large smile my way and gave me energy. I could feel his energy penetrating me.

"Has there ever been anyone who has used a hundred percent of their brain power?"

"Yes, there is only one being that can do that. That being is God. God is all-knowing, He is constant energy, He is the universe, and when our souls reach heaven they will be able to use all the resources of the universe one hundred percent. Because heaven is on a higher vibration plane, and it is full of love and understanding, God gives our souls the ability to be all-knowing and loving as He is. Everything is intertwined, interconnected, in such a way that our body is the universe, and the universe is our body."

As I thought about it, the conversation made more and more sense to me because we were in fact created from the earth itself. The body and the earth and universe were mirror images of each other. I felt as if a lightbulb had just turned on within me. I looked at the ocean and felt complete appreciation for it. I also felt complete love and appreciation for Nathan. He was a wise soul and extraordinary human being.

"How did you come to realize all of this?"

"When I was in Spain, I spent a lot of time in nature. I had an unbelievable experience when I was on a hilltop one day. I was sleeping outside one night, and I woke up to birds chirping and the wind blowing. I was enjoying the morning air, and as the sun rose in the east over the green hilltop, I had this amazing discovery: We are all connected, and every thing and every living breathing entity in this great universe is one."

"How did you realize this though?" I wanted him to be more specific.

"I realized it because I felt love. I felt an immense appreciation for the beauty that was surrounding me, for the beauty within myself. I was full of life and energy, and then it dawned on me as I saw the bright yellow-orange sun come over the mountaintop giving the sleepy hill life. The sun had so much energy that it made an earthly awakening. My heart began to beat faster in my chest. The body of earth is in fact our body, and all of the elements of the universe are embodied within us, but nobody takes the time to recognize this. I had a complete awakening on that hilltop that morning. It was amazing. Whenever, I get down, or depressed about the ignorance and the negativity of the world, I think about that moment and it gives me peace. It fills me with love."

Truth #8—We all possess the entire universe within our being. The human body is a mirror image of the earth. One must appreciate the earth as they appreciate their body because they are one in the same. The spirit of the universe is constant with the spirit of our soul. Once you recognize this, you can tap into the peace and love that is inside you at all times.

"I was wondering why you are so grounded and now I got my answer," I told Nathan as I looked into his hazel eyes. The sun busted through the gray clouds and illuminated our faces.

"When you are full of this love, you become the real you and you have absolute faith in yourself that all your dreams can come true. I wasn't always this grounded," he said, "but the one thing that always keeps me in check is the appreciation and love for everything and everyone around me. Once you have that light inside, you can accomplish anything. And you can feel happiness and peace at all times. It's really an awesome way to live. You must embrace the fullness of this love at all times, and when you feel yourself losing energy from the negativities around you, you must stop and get reenergized by appreciating the love of the universe. Because you are made of the universe, appreciating the beauty of the universe is really appreciating the mirror image of your-self, you will always feel beautiful, and always feel love."

"I never looked at it that way." I was amazed by this.

"Madison, I know that this is an enlightening experience and that it takes time to let it register. I am the universe, and the universe is me. Isn't that amazing?" He put his hand on my arm and looked at me deeply.

"You are amazing," I said to him. He beamed.

Diana and Brian were listening to the entire conversation. Their faces were glowing as the wind blew through our hair. I looked at Diana and Brian, as Brian smiled back at me.

"So you need to appreciate the love of the universe and by appreci-ating it you will feel love and be able to accomplish anything?" Diana asked Nathan.

"Yes, that's correct."

Diana looked at the seashell that Brian once held to his ear. "I can appreciate this shell, and how it came into existence, but how can you appreciate the things that are bad in the universe? Like cancer and mur-der and death? How can you still feel love when all of these bad things are happening in the world?" Diana was concerned, as she looked to Nathan for an explanation.

Nathan collected his thoughts and cleared his throat. "There are bad things in this world and they happen for a reason, for a greater good. They are there to make us stronger, to make us learn something about ourselves. All of the horrible things that happen to us shape us into better people. They force us to listen to the universe. Think of it this way, if the world was always peaceful and harmonious and we never had to experience anything bad, how could we learn to appreciate the good things that we have? We would simply take them for granted and never value their worth. The world would be so accustomed to every-thing being good, our souls would not progress or evolve into the souls that we were meant to be. Our greatest challenges are our greatest teach-ers. Without the challenges in life, we would never grow and prosper or reach our full potential."

"We learned about that during the misunderstood truth," Brian interjected.

"If we were never tested on our beliefs, or forced to change our thinking, we would never reach our true purpose," I said to Diana.

"Yeah, I guess you're right," she said, as she admired the shell. We all stopped talking for a moment and observed our surroundings. I appreciated the ocean with all of its waves and grains of sand, and the surrounding trees, and the seagulls, pigeons, and sea oats. It was beautiful, and I thought about how all of these different entities of the universe are a reflection of me. The sturdiness of the land, the heartbeat of the sun, the infinite wisdom of the mind, then a thought dawned on me.

"What are the eyes of the universe? What part of the universe is the eye?" I asked Nathan.

"I want you to figure it out," he said.

"I don't know, I'm stumped, and you guys have to help me. What is a reflection of my eyes? What is the one entity that is able to see and capture everything in the universe at any given moment?" I looked up and noticed that the clouds had moved to the west and the sun was no longer covered with grayness. It was now surrounded by the most beautiful blue. This blue did not only surround the sun, it surrounded everything.

Then I realized something profound. "Like the eyes, the sky sees everything. It encompasses everything and it oversees all of the entities of the universe. And like the eyes, when it sleeps it is dark, and when it awakens there is light. This is true because of the heartbeat of the universe being the sun. If one has a heartbeat form within, then they will see the light. But even the sky's eyes need to rest at night. That is when the universe is turned away from the heartbeat so that it can become rejuvenated again. When the sun or heartbeat rises again over the horizon, the eye of the sky can open and awaken to see a brand-new day. So the eye of the universe is the sky. The heartbeat, the brain, the eyes, the lungs, all work together in unison. But like the universe as a whole that never sleeps all at one time, neither does the brain sleep completely.

There is still activity going on in the brain, because even at night there is still activity in the universe." I looked at Nathan for validation.

"That is right, Madison, the eye is the sky. The sky witnesses everything." We all looked at each other and smiled. The wind blew through our lungs just as it blew through the trees and filled us with our breath. As that happened Brian's face lit up with energy.

"I got it!" he shouted with delight. "The sky is the eye, and our breath is the wind! We are constantly reminded of this because there is always a wind, sometimes there are higher winds sometimes lower winds, but it is always there, as our breath is always there to keep us alive. Without the wind the trees could not live, and if the trees are our lungs, without breath they could not function."

"Wow, that's right, Brian, you hit the nail on the head," Nathan said to him. A proud look came across his face.

"This is awesome, man." Brian was ecstatic. Diana was still looking at the shell, trying to comprehend it all as she played with the gothic silver necklace that hung around her neck.

"So let me get this straight. The rock, soil, and land are our skin and bone; the lakes, oceans, and tributaries are our veins; the trees and plants are our lungs; the sun is our heart; the sky is our eyes; the wind is our breath, but we are forgetting one thing? What are our muscles?"

"That's the one element that we haven't touched on, Diana. Can you tell us?" Nathan gazed at her.

"Well, our muscles wrap around our bones, and they give us strength and substance and are fueled by proteins, vitamins, and nutrients. So our muscles must have something to do with our skin and bones, which is the land. But they have to add strength to the land."

"You're on the right track. Keep going," Nathan told her.

"I have no idea," she said as she played with her necklace, trying to gain insight. "The hard, strong elements that add value to the universe. Hmm…"

"What else do muscles need to get stronger?"

Diana thought about it long and hard. "They need vitamins, minerals, and proteins, but they also have to be worked to get bigger and stronger." She looked at Nathan, wondering if she was wrong. "They need exercise. Is that right?"

"Yes! Let me ask you a question, Diana. What is the hardest, strongest, most beautiful natural resource in the world?"

"I thought rocks and land are our bones?" She looked confused.

"They are," he said. "Okay, let me rephrase that. What is the hardest stone?"

"What does that have to do with anything?" she asked.

"These stones are created in the earth and they have been worked and exercised with years of proteins and minerals from the universe," he said.

"Well, I guess a diamond is the most precious stone?"

"Exactly," Nathan proclaimed. "It's also the hardest and strongest, most illustrious stone that is created from the earth. It is valued for its strength, luster, and magnificence. The carbon proteins have exercised for thousands of years and built up to create a diamond. Why do you think when someone has developed their muscles they feel as hard as rock? Precious stones are the muscles of the universe. The other elements that are the muscles of the earth are platinum, gold, silver, diamonds, sapphires, emeralds, rubies, and so on.

"The more muscles you develop in your body, the healthier and fitter you become. Your body has a greater value, and the earth has a greater value because of these strong solid elements. That silver necklace around your neck is actually a well-developed muscle of your body. Think about it: Why did jewelry hold such importance for kings and queens?" Brian, Diana, and I looked at each other questioningly. "Because by wearing gold and diamonds they felt stronger, more powerful, and more elite. The muscles of the body can be as developed as a diamond, or as solid as a piece of gold. The muscles of the universe are the precious stones and elements of the earth," Nathan exclaimed.

"That's amazing," I said. *That's something that I never would have thought about, let alone understood,* I thought.

We stared at the surrounding landscape and realized that we were the universe. The four of us walked up to the shore of the ocean getting our feet wet with the cold salty water. Diana splashed Brian with water. Staring into the blue water of the ocean, I saw my reflection in the water and smiled. I felt my skin, my bones, my eyes, my muscles, my lungs breathing in and out, my heart beating and my mind working. I could not believe what I had just learned.

"What do you guys have to say about all this?" Nathan was looking at us intently.

Brian, Diana, and I looked at each other and smiled. At once we said, "Keystone, True, and Jeremiah too." The four of us laughed and smiled on the beach as our bodies were reflected in the ocean.

Life is everywhere. The earth is throbbing with it, it's like music. The plants, the creatures, the ones we see, the ones we don't see, it's like one, big, pulsating symphony.
—Diane Frolov and Andrew Schneider, *Northern Exposure,* "Zarya," 1994

XI

KEYSTONE, TRUE, AND JEREMIAH

I woke up and felt my body as the entire universe. I no longer felt like a different species apart from the world because I realized I held the key to the entire world, and now I was able to unleash it at will. I possessed the entire love of the universe within. It was magnificent.

I thought about Nathan, and I immediately wondered about his feelings toward me. He seemed too good to be true.

In a few hours I would be at the week's anticipated baseball game, and I thought about how much my mentality had grown since the game had presented itself to me six days earlier. I thought about how on that day I had allowed all my negative thoughts to get the best of me after talking to the Plague. Now, I could never imagine myself feeling that way after what I had learned this week. I felt completely alive, and this beautiful maze of knowledge had brought me to realize who I was, what my core was, and what I possessed inside. I held the love of the universe within me, and that was something not many people realized through-out their lives. What a shame that was—even if everybody in the world were told that inside of them was infinite love, most people wouldn't believe it or even understand what it meant.

The negativity of the world made me sad. There were too many people who misunderstood the concept of infinite love. *When people are ready to understand the concept, they will,* I thought. *There are still so many things I have yet to learn, and I am thrilled to keep walking through this maze of knowledge that is life.*

I was supposed to meet Brian, Diana, and Nathan in the quad, and from there we would meet the Plague and her other cronies at the baseball field at one o'clock. I felt foolish calling Rachel the Plague. It turned out, she really wasn't the Plague at all. The bubonic plague that had killed thousands of people in the world was eventually for greater good, because from that horror came many health regulations and laws that made the world a healthier place. And I already felt like a healthier person for having known her. I was full of anticipation again, and I allowed myself to fully feel this enthusiasm. It felt terrific. I had no idea what to expect and I just rolled with it, like I had been doing all week.

I walked toward the quad with my anticipation running high. I saw Diana walking from her direction, Brian walking from his direction, and Nathan walking from his direction. We all came together at the same point right in the center of the quad. This was just the stopping point leading toward the direction we were now meant to experience together: the baseball game.

We said our hellos as Diana looked uneasy. "What's wrong?" Brian asked her.

"I've haven't watched one of my dad's games since I was a kid. I'm nervous. I won't know what to tell him."

"Just go with the flow," Brian told her. "Don't worry about it, it will be fine."

"Yeah, I guess you're right, but if my dad sees me in the crowd, he might think I'm bad luck or something," she said.

"He'll probably be happy to see you there," I said.

"I don't know about that." Diana looked away as uncertainty crossed her face.

"C'mon, let's go. Are we ready?" Nathan asked, looking at Diana.

"Ready as I'll ever be," she said. We began walking and I glanced over at Nathan and smiled. He returned the smile and I wanted to hug him so badly. I hugged him in spirit and I knew he felt it.

We headed toward the baseball field; Diana grew more and more nervous. We made some stupid jokes and tried to get her mind off it. We finally arrived at the baseball stadium as we saw news vans, journalists, fans, and camera crews all trying to pile into the stadium. We saw Rachel with her two girlfriends waiting by one of the gates. She was holding our tickets, and she looked up and instantly made eye contact with me. She ran over toward me and hugged me with excitement.

"I'm so happy you could come. Thank you so much; this means a lot to Jeff." She paused. "It means a lot to me too." Her voice cracked. She was sincere, and for the first time I felt terrible about the way I had felt about her. I felt so foolish, and without a word I begged for her forgiveness as I hugged her back. Rachel's two friends stood by the gate examining the situation. Clearly overdressed for a baseball game, they looked like they were headed to a dance club. But I tried not to judge this time. Everyone has their own idea of how they want to appear to the world; if being overdressed at a baseball game is the way they want to be, who am I to say anything?

I went over to say hello to them and to introduce them to Diana and Nathan. They already knew Brian, of course, because he was Jeff's roommate. The two girls looked Diana up and down, clearly not impressed with her camouflage shorts and anarchy tee shirt. They sized her up and cringed at her appearance. Diana didn't notice. Her mind was on her father and the game.

We went inside the stadium and found seats that were reserved for us in the second row. Rachel and Brian said their hellos to Jeff's family. Everyone was nervous about Jeff pitching. There were many pro scouts in attendance, and this game would be the deciding factor as to whether he would get drafted by a pro team. I could sense the nervousness in the air. The air was thick and humid; the midday sun was beaming down on us. There was no breeze. It was just plain hot.

We settled into plastic blue seats as the players took the first and third baselines for the singing of the national anthem. They put their hats over their hearts, as Diana gawked at her father. He was a short, rather stocky man with a large midsection hanging way over his baseball pants, a balding head, and a very serious demeanor. I could feel his energy and determination in the stands. You could tell he meant business. There was no smile, no friendly kindness in his eyes. He was simply stoic, poised, and determined to win this game.

As the young girl sang the national anthem in a cruise ship voice, finally a light breeze picked up off the field and blew through the coach's thinning gray hair. In his tenure at Braxton he'd had a seven hundred winning percentage and had taken his teams to the playoffs all but one year. This year he was determined to win the college division three championship. He knew he had the talent. The starting lineup was strong with home-run power, a solid defense, and a deep bench. But he was counting on Jeff Greenberg to pitch the game of his life. Jeff had pitched a number of shutout baseball games in his career, allowing only a couple of hits, striking out a school-record fifteen batters in one game, and possessing an earned run average just under two. His control was the issue today; if he could focus on his strikeouts, they were sure to win.

On humid days, the ball jumps off the bat, a fact of which he was well aware. The only other issue was to keep the ball down and make the opposition hit ground balls into double plays if he got in a jam. There was so much anticipation and nervousness, it made the humidity ten times thicker.

When the girl finished the national anthem, the announcer said, "Play ball!" The crowd clapped and cheered as Brian whistled loudly. Rachel was fidgeting with her hair, clearly anxious for Jeff to throw his first pitch. He was on the mound warming up and she screamed, "Go Jeff!"

As the coach walked up the field and headed for the dugout, he looked up into the cheering crowd. Then he stopped in his tracks and looked right at Diana in the second row. He maintained his poise, didn't wave or smile. He simply looked at her. Diana looked back at him. The moment must have seemed like an eternity to them. It was awkward. Then her father walked into the dugout as if nothing happened.

"You see, he didn't even notice me. I knew he wouldn't like me here; he thinks I'm a jinx."

"No, he doesn't," I protested, "he's just concentrating on the game, I'm sure he's happy that you came to watch."

"No, he's not, he hates it. He hates me." She put her hands over her face.

"That's not true; he's happy, I'm sure of it." Diana didn't believe me; she sat silently as they announced the leadoff hitter for the opposing team.

Jeff continued to warm up. He kicked up his leg and threw the ball so fast it was barely visible. He looked confident and strong. He had complete control. *Wow, he can really throw,* I thought. The anticipation and eagerness grew as the first batter stepped into the box. His short muscular legs dug in, he took some practice swings and eyeballed Jeff at the mound. Jeff looked at the sign from the catcher, nodded his head slightly, and threw a perfect fastball right down the middle. "Strike!" the umpire yelled and signaled. And the game was underway.

I noticed that the blond annoying guy I'd met in the cafeteria was at shortstop. He had a determined, almost mean look on his face as he looked at the catcher's signs. He kept spitting in his glove and rubbing it to get a good grip on a ground ball if it was hit his way. His thick stubby hands kept adjusting his crotch. After many spits and moving the dirt around him with his spiked shoes, the next pitch was delivered. Jeff took a different grip on the laces, creating more spin on the ball. It was a breaking ball and it cut sharply over the plate, but the batter took the pitch a little low for ball one.

Diana's face was still tense, as I looked over at her and saw the wheels spinning in her preoccupied mind. I could tell she was still thinking about her dad. I wanted to tell her that he was happy she came to watch the game. But I really didn't know if that was the case. He didn't look like a nice man, and maybe he was angry that she was there. Why did he make her feel unwanted? That was something I could not answer. I focused on the blue sky overhead and remembered that the sky is eye of the universe.

The batter swung late at the next pitch and fouled it off into the stands as people scrambled to catch the ball. A young man wearing an oversized Braxton jersey caught the white ball with his bare hand and held it up proudly while his friends applauded. The count was now one ball and two strikes. Jeff was in control of the situation as he prepared for the payoff pitch. It was important to retire the first batter because that sets the tone for the entire game. The windup and the delivery was solid. The batter was clearly looking for a fastball, the question was, could the batter catch up to a ninety-five-mile-an-hour pitch? Jeff smoked it past him as the batter desperately tried to catch up to the heat. He swung right through it, as his entire body was still in motion. Strike three, the batter was out. The catcher threw the ball sharply to third as the ball went around the horn.

The crowd roared with enthusiasm as many fans stood up from their plastic chairs and cheered. Rachel was the first fan to her feet, and she jumped up and down, shouting at the top of her lungs. "Yeah, baby! Whoo-hoo! Yes!" The tall, stoic pitcher kept his composure on the mound, not even cracking a smile. Brian and Nathan were enjoying the moment, as was I, impressed with Jeff's pitching. Diana was still edgy looking up from her nervous nail biting. She was unaware of what just happened.

Jeff struck out the next batter and got his last man out with a routine ground ball to second. And with a throw to the first baseman, the top of the first inning was in the books. As Rachel cheered loudly for Jeff, the team jogged off the field and into the dugout.

The game slowly transpired into a pitching dual. Either team had only accumulated four hits into the top of the fifth inning leaving men stranded on the bases. Jeff had brought his good stuff to the game today, and had retired six of the last seven batters. His curveball was sharp, and his off speed stuff was making the batters look foolish. He would finish the batter off by making the guy swing at something out of the strike zone, or at a sinking curveball that they would hit into the ground. He had studied the scouting report and knew which guys would go fishing for a high fastball, or which guys to pitch inside to and then get them swinging at something low and away. Pitching was a science and Jeff made it look easy. The press box was full of scouts and reporters analyzing every pitch, and Jeff was really showing off today. Rachel was so proud, as her face beamed watching him on the mound. His parents were relatively quiet. They were very nervous and it showed in their tense shoulders.

I would occasionally look over at Nathan and he would glance at me and smile. He was such a great guy, and I felt grateful to be around him. The sun was dipping in and out of the clouds; it was so sticky that beads of sweat rolled down the players' brows as they took off their hats to wipe the moisture from their foreheads. The sweat on Jeff's upper lip was clearly visible as he concentrated on the catcher's signs, shaking his head slightly at first, then coming to a compromise. The heart of Amherst's order was due up next. Jeff had to be very stingy with his pitches to move on. He also needed his teammates' bats to come alive if he wanted a chance to win. Jeff was pitching a gem, but so was Amherst's pitcher. This was a critical time in the game.

The pitch count was relatively low, but the humidity was taking its toll as Jeff started to lose his sharpness. The first batter hit a ground ball deep in the infield, and the third baseman had to make an off-balance throw to first. The throw was not in time and Amherst had a runner on first. Amherst had some life now, and Jeff was clearly upset, kicking dirt on the mound. The next batter had home-run power, and the key was to keep the ball low. One costly mistake here could lose the game. The catcher called time-out as he charged the mound to talk to Jeff. They covered their mouths with their gloves so there wasn't any lipreading from the other team. The catcher wanted to make sure they were on the same page about the next pitch.

Rachel's leg was shaking as she took deep breaths. I could see the love in her eyes for Jeff, and that was something that I could never come between. No matter how attractive I thought he was or what kind of connection I thought I felt with him, they were meant to be together at this moment in time, and I could tell their love was real. The truth was I didn't have a clue about Jeff, and I never would. People are together for a reason, and whatever I imagined in my mind about our chance meeting that day in the cafeteria was simply that: imaginary. I smiled to myself as the sun peeked through the clouds and illuminated home plate. I could almost hear Jeff's heart beating from where I was sitting.

He was ready to pitch, and the first throw was a strike right down the middle of the plate. Jeff immediately looked at the runner on first base, trying to hold him on. The batter stepped out of the batter's box, taking many practice swings and looking over at the third base coach to read the signs. Maybe the hit and run was on. The next pitch was hit sharply to the shortstop, as he threw to second for one out, and the second baseman threw to first and turned the double play beautifully. It was a five-four-three double play. That was just what the fans wanted to see as they applauded and Jeff breathed a sigh of relief. Now he faced the next batter, who luckily swung at the first pitch. He was thinking home run all the way, but he got under the ball and skied it deep to right field where the right fielder backed up and caught the deep drive near the warning track. The top of the fifth was over. Still a zero-zero tie ball game. Jeff was pitching like a star. Rachel was blowing kisses at him as he walked slowly to the dugout, and the fans cheered his great performance.

Diana did not look happy. The pressure seemed too much to bear as she thought about her father's stomach in knots. She hardly said two words since the game started. Brian and Nathan were enjoying themselves eating hot dogs and peanuts, and booing the opposition every so often, then standing up to cheer at a great play. There is no better sound than the crack of the bat. I was having fun. The bottom of the Braxton order was due up next and we really needed to get something going to take a little pressure off Jeff. The first batter struck out swinging, then the next batter lined out to the shortstop, and Jeff was due up next. Maybe he could get a hit here to help his own cause. Or even a walk, anything to swing the momentum our way. Jeff struck out swinging. The fans grew quiet. It was anyone's game.

The six and seventh innings went by with only two hits. It was still zero-zero going into the top of the eighth. The fans were getting a little restless as they longed for more action. Jeff was still pitching strong, but one mistake could cost him the game here. One hanging breaking ball could be the deciding factor, and before you knew it, the game could be out of reach. The coach walked out to the mound very slowly to talk to

Jeff to see how his arm was holding up. He needed to know if Jeff had anything left in the tank. Jeff nodded, knowing that it was his game to win. The crowed cheered in support of their star pitcher as they clapped and yelled Jeff's name loudly.

Diana stared at her father on the mound with his player. He was clearly concerned about Jeff. He looked at his ace with pride and appreciation as if Jeff were his own son. The situation was strange and painful for her to watch. After a few moments she excused herself to the bathroom. I wasn't sure if she wanted me to join her, but by the look on her face, she wanted to be alone for a while and I nodded at her. I allowed myself to feel sorry for her. I needed to feel her pain, and then detach from it and let it go. I knew that being at this game was a great step for Diana to take; if it had been a week earlier there was no way she would have been here. I thought about her dream of bridging the gap, and this was a start for her inching closer to her father, the coach, however painful it was. I knew she was feeling great pain, walking through the crowded stadium, and that was exactly what she needed to feel.

The meeting on the mound was over and play resumed. After walking the first batter he faced, then giving up a single up the middle to the next hitter, Jeff retired the next three batters, leaving two runners on. Jeff had done everything he could to keep them in the game. The coaching staff, the rest of the players on the team, and the entire stadium of fans knew that it was time for the hitters to get some runs if they were going to win this game. That was what everyone was praying for. The first batter hit a fly ball into shallow center field for out number one. The crowed sighed loudly, and became more agitated and impatient.

The next batter was the annoying shortstop, Troy Gunnison. He dug in the batter's box, took his stance bending at the knees, and took strike one on the outside corner. He turned around and complained to the umpire that the ball was outside.

"Do you need glasses, man? That ball was nowhere near the corner!" he yelled at the umpire.

"You know that you can't argue balls and strikes, son. I suggest you keep your mouth shut," the umpire scolded. Troy pouted his lips and stomped his foot like a spoiled brat, hitting the head of his bat on home plate. He dug in the batter's box again and swung through ball one chasing a high pitch rising quickly near his chest. Again he clanked the head of his bat on home plate in frustration. Next pitch, he took a wicked swing with all his might but could not catch up to it. He struck out. Troy kicked the dirt and threw his bat into the dugout, swearing, spitting, and cursing to himself as the crowd booed his antics.

There were two out in the bottom of the ninth, still tied zero-zero. Diana came back from her bathroom break. "Did I miss anything?"

"Two outs in the bottom of the ninth." I told her.

"Oh, great. See, I am a jinx. They're going to lose this game."

"They still have a chance," I said, trying to be optimistic. "They could win it in extra innings." The opposing pitcher was getting fatigued. He had pitched the entire game and his arm had to be hurting. His face was red and sweaty, and his forehead wrinkled in pain.

The next batter was third baseman Brad Keystone. He wasn't the greatest hitter and he lacked power, but he was a strong defensive player and had good speed. It was his time to produce. He stood in the batter's box and took ball one high. He foul-tipped ball two for a strike. The count was one and one. Then he watched as ball two was in the dirt. It was two balls and a strike. Next, ball three almost sailed over the catcher's head. The pitcher was clearly losing his control, and was overexerting himself. He was really stretching it. His coach and his catcher had a meeting on the mound, and told him to just try to throw a strike. The next pitch was outside, for ball four. He walked him. Keystone's patience at the plate had paid off. Keystone was on first base with two out, bottom of the ninth.

The next batter was catcher Kyle True. Kyle had home-run power but had been in a hitting slump lately, only three for his last twenty-two at bats. It didn't look good. But with the first pitch, Kyle lined a solid single up the left side. The crowed roared with excitement as the entire stadium was now on their feet. Rachel and her cronies were jumping up and down, bellowing at the top of their lungs. Brian and Nathan clapped noisily.

There were runners on first and second, two out in the bottom of the ninth. One hit would win the ball game. The next batter in the lineup would have been Jeff in the ninth spot. Now the coach had an important decision to make. Did he keep Jeff in the ball game for the tenth inning or pull him, and put in a pinch hitter to take his place? Jeff was not the best hitter or runner. It was a crucial situation. He was going to put in a pinch hitter most likely.

Diana looked at her dad in the dugout talking to his other coaches. Her face looked sad, as if she wanted to help him in this crucial situation but was helpless. She felt like a jinx, and she was powerless to do anything about it. She sat still for a moment, looking at her surroundings. She concentrated and looked up with a renewed expression. Her attitude had changed, and I could sense her getting stronger. She then looked at the players on first and second base. She read the back of their jerseys. Then slowly she read: Keystone and True.

"Where have I heard that before?"

"Heard what before?" I replied.

"Keystone and True," she repeated loudly, and that got Brian's and Nathan's attention. "Keystone, True," she said it again. Then it dawned on us all at the same time as our jaws dropped. We said it in unison, "Keystone, True, and Jeremiah too!"

"Oh my God," Diana exclaimed. "I have to tell my dad to put in Jeremiah. Who's Jeremiah, Brian?"

"I don't know, Diana. There is no Jeremiah on the team."

"No, there has to be a Jeremiah." She was full of light and energy. "I have to go tell my father." She ran through the stadium and into the dugout. The coach was talking to his coaching staff as she bolted, darted, and ran through the clubhouse and into the dugout. She was panting by now, as she yelled with all her might.

"You have to put in Jeremiah." Her father turned quickly, knowing that voice sounded familiar. He was shocked.

"What are you doing here? Go back to your seat, now!" he scolded her.

"No, you have to put in Jeremiah!"

144

"You don't know what you are talking about." He ridiculed her. "Go back to your seat! You're not allowed to be here."

"Put in Jeremiah!" she pleaded with all her might. The fire was burning in her father's eyes.

"You don't know what you're talking about; there is no Jeremiah on the team," He shouted. "Now get out of here, Diana, that's an order!"

"I will not leave until you put in Jeremiah!" she persisted.

"Have you gone crazy? There is no Jeremiah here." Diana's face grew helpless again. Tears filled her eyes.

"Get out, Diana, I will not say it again!" he shouted. There was some rustling on the bench, and a short, dark-haired player walked closer. Then someone shouted from the back of the dugout, "Put Jerry in!" The short player inched closer to the coach.

"My real name is Jeremiah," he told the coach. His name was Jerry Fragolio.

The coach was furious.

"You haven't played all game, you're the back-up catcher, you can't hit," the coach said.

"Just give me a chance," Jerry said. The coach looked at his daughter. He was shocked at her antics and amazed that she knew the name Jeremiah. He looked at Jerry, then back at Diana. She was no longer helpless or powerless, her face and body were full of strength as she smiled at her father. The coach looked at her, then at Jerry.

"Get your ass in there." He looked at Diana again sternly. Jerry got his bat and batting helmet, and took to the plate. The coach walked out to the umpire and showed his card for the pinch hitter. Diana watched from the dugout.

Brad Keystone was on second base, Kyle True was on first base, and Jeremiah was at the plate. The entire crowd was holding its breath. It was so silent you could hear a pin drop. They were wondering why Jerry Fragolio was in the game. Clearly, there were other pinch hitters on the bench that were better in this kind of situation. The coach didn't even look confident in his decision. He couldn't even bear to watch.

The first pitch Jeremiah swung through, which made him look silly. The crowd groaned. The coach blinked his eyes long and hard. The next pitch, Jerry almost caught up to, but he fouled it off his bat straight into the stands behind home plate. The humidity was electric as the clouds rolled in. There was a thunderstorm brewing in the distance. The grey clouds were thick and powerful and the wind picked up slightly as the temperature dropped a few degrees. There was so much moisture in the air, I could feel the stickiness all over my body.

I watched Jeremiah in the batter's box. He was a small guy with curly jet black hair. He had powerful legs and strong forearms. He dug in deep. The pitcher looked at the runner on second. Keystone had good speed at second. No balls, two strikes, bottom of the ninth. The pitcher stepped off the rubber, took three deep breaths, and wiped the sweat off his brow. He eyeballed the runner on second. Diana looked at Jeremiah, as her whole body was alive. Alive in a way it had never been. She was electric.

The pitcher got into his delivery, there was the windup, and the pitch—Jeremiah swung with all his might. With a crack of the bat, there was a drive, swung on, and belted, deep to left. The wind was carrying it, it might be, it could be...The left fielder raced back to the warning track, he timed his leap. He jumped as high as he could. The ball still carried in the air. The left fielder reached the pinnacle of his soaring leap. With one swoop of the glove the left fielder grabbed for the spinning ball, and the wind howled as the clouds crashed in over the stadium. That ball was gone. It was a home run. The roar of the crowd was deafening. The crowd jumped out of their seats, and raced the field. This was Diana's moment. She watched Keystone, then True, and finally her angel Jeremiah. In a stampede, the entire Braxton bench rushed the field to pick up little Jerry Fragolio. They put him on their shoulders and carried him around the field. It truly was Keystone, True, and Jeremiah too!

The coach ran out to the field to pat Jeremiah on the head as he was smiling from ear to ear. Who would have thought that a back-up catcher who's hitting average was one seventy-eight would have hit a game-winning home run over the left field fence to beat Amherst three to zero in a thrilling victory? Brian, Nathan, and I were standing and cheering as we watched the players carry Jeremiah around the field. We could not believe what had just transpired. Brian leaned over to tell me, "I can't believe that Diana's instinct told her that Keystone, True, and Jeremiah would win the ball game. She really listened to her thoughts, and maybe if she hadn't told us about them yesterday and actually brought her premonition to life this never would have happened.

"When I walked to the beach yesterday and saw her writing those three words in the sand, I had no idea what they were or what they meant. And the funny thing is neither did she. But she believed that there was something significant about those three words that popped into her head, and she wrote them in the sand. This was a miracle."

Nathan leaned into the conversation, trying to talk through all the cheering fans. "That is why it is so important to believe in your instincts and your premonitions, even if they don't make any sense to you at the time. The universe has a funny way of letting you know they are meaningful. If she never brought her premonition to life, or shrugged it off as nonsense, this never would have happened. She easily could have thought she was crazy and discarded it as meaningless. Because she listened to her instinct and valued it as having some kind of substance she brought it into reality, and the premonition happened right before her eyes. The coolest thing about it is that she recognized it unfolding, and went to her father and told him. By following her instinct she bridged the gap that was between her and the coach."

This was such an awakening for me; I didn't know what to say. Brian and I were still shell-shocked as we gazed upon the wild celebration on the field. The happiness and love throughout the stadium was so moving, it brought tears to my eyes. The players were jumping for joy, giving high fives, and patting each other on the head and backsides. It was truly awesome. Rachel ran onto the field and jumped up and swung her legs around Jeff in an embrace as they hugged and kissed passionately. This was the greatest moment of love and happiness I had ever seen. I was moved, as my heart grew heavy and eyes watery.

I watched from the seats as the coach congratulated his players. In the dugout, Diana was still smiling. She looked alive and full of energy and happiness as she watched the players and her father celebrate. It was a profound moment for Diana.

After the celebrating subsided, her father walked into the dugout and saw Diana sitting there beaming. He was smiling at her and she was smiling back. This kind of interaction between them reminded her of when she was a little girl, the apple of his eye. It was familiar and comforting. She hadn't felt him being proud of her in years. Although he didn't say any words, she could feel the warmness from his eyes. He walked closer to her, still smiling. They embraced long and hard, as his eyes filled with tears.

"How did you know to put in Jerry? How did you know?" he asked in astonishment.

"I just had a feeling. I just had a feeling," she said softly, as tears of joy and sorrow rolled down her cheeks. He pulled her closer. All he could say through his tears of joy was "Thank you." They continued to embrace as the stadium was roaring.

I watched this from my seat in the second row, and I was moved to the depths of my soul. Brian and Nathan seemed to share the same thoughts as we put our hands together with a strong connection. While holding each other's hands, we looked at each other happily.

> Truth #9—*Once you become one with the spirit of your true life force, the miracles of the universe start to present themselves to you. Life becomes an enchanting unfolding of miracles.*

So many people go to their own graves,
without ever hearing their own music.

—Anonymous

XII

ON THE STRINGS OF VIOLINS

Today was the day we would return to philosophy class with our newfound truths tucked tightly under our arms. The week of intrigue had come to a pinnacle, and I was now wondering how there could be anything more profound than what I had witnessed yesterday. Diana's instincts had come into her consciousness and turned a baseball game into an insightful and surreal event. I still could not believe what happened and how it happened. It was purely mystical.

I can remember the first class of people watching, the loud groans of confused students, and the absolute chaos when we were told that we had to unravel the nine truths of life. Now these truths seemed as if they had always been a part of me, but I'd just failed to recognize them. I had already discovered the coincidences that happen, but I had no idea what they meant or how to make them happen more regularly. We not only unraveled the truths about life, but we unraveled the truths of ourselves. Looking back on the week, I was amazed at how far we'd all come. Everything was truly intertwined together and although at times I felt scared and confused, there was always something or someone that came along to lead us into the right direction.

I didn't understand how our instincts worked. The thought of using a third eye to lead us toward our path on earth had never crossed my mind before this week. Or that we all had an insecurity that we use on others to gain energy, or that there were forces in nature that helped us gain or lose clarity. Or that everyone had a core they had to follow to fulfill their life purpose, and that the only way one reaches his or her

149

core was by using the love of the universe, and that the universe was inside each and every one of us, but we had to learn to tap into it. The motivation that made our core a reality was using the love we already possess.

I was curious what Professor Jacobs would tell us about these truths. I thought about Nathan and wished I could see him again. But something told me I would. As I walked toward the grassy knoll, the sky was the eye of the universe. I felt the heartbeat of the universe illuminating my retina causing my eye to see the world clearly. The more I realized that inside of me, I possess the universe, the more I became one with it, causing the coincidences of life to happen more frequently and more importantly. Diana's mystical message was all the insight and validation I needed to verify that what I have learned this week was not a figment of my imagination, but a factual, beautiful discovery that I will cherish, and for which I will forever be grateful.

The question was, could I utilize these truths throughout the rest of my life even if the other people I encountered didn't recognize them? Especially if the most important people in my life like my family and friends weren't aware of them? I understood that not everybody can enroll in a philosophy class or experience these truths without being ready to alter their perceptions of life.

Let's face it: Most people are not open-minded enough and don't have the mentality to follow these truths even if the truths are told to them and experienced firsthand. That would be the obstacle, and if Dr. Jacobs did not address this issue in class today, I would ask him about it.

But if I could maintain a high enough vibrational energy level, I supposed that the right people would find me. Just like the various teachers found us at exactly the right time we needed them. Just when we were at our worst, most confused, and isolated state of mind, someone would come along and give us the knowledge and the understanding that we needed. The key was to keep these truths in our consciousness and maintain our energy long enough.

I arrived at the grassy knoll and sat down. The smell of freshly cut grass made me think of my childhood—of grass stains on my knees, of

150

running and playing, of fanciful imaginations. I never would have imagined that I could experience life this way. You never know what you can become until you are willing to put yourself out on a limb and climb the twisted, tangled branches that lead you to where you need to be. Watching the other students gather around me, I saw Brian and Diana walking toward me and they looked refreshed and happy. Diana was actually smiling and laughing with Brian. I almost didn't recognize her. She looked beautiful. And to think, a week ago she was the mopey girl who made the sidewalk wallow in her pain. She now looked alive and vibrant. I felt a tickle in my throat when I smiled at them. They sat down next to me, and we didn't have to say anything. Our smiling faces did all the communicating. These two different people had become my closest and dearest friends in a matter of a week. I am amazed by them.

We waited patiently for Dr. Jacobs to arrive. As I took a look around, I noticed that a few of the obnoxious students from last week were nowhere in sight. The confused guy with the shaggy long hair had obviously dropped the class. A few other guys and girls were not present either.

I looked at Diana and thought about how at first, she wanted to drop the course too. Looking back I was so relieved she didn't. She would have missed out on the opportunity of knowing Brian and me, but most importantly, she would not have discovered that her true core is art, and she never would have found a way to bridge the gap with her father.

Dr. Jacobs walked up to the podium with the sun to his back again. His faced scanned the students.

"Hello, everybody. I see there are fewer of you here today. That was to be expected. There are always about eight or nine students who decide they don't want to discover the truths, and that is perfectly fine. Not everyone is on the same spiritual path. Those people who decide not to change and discover new knowledge tend to live that way their entire lives. That is the particular life path they are traveling. However, those of us who understand and value that there is more to life than meets the eye, will find others whose mentality is the same."

He answered my question right away, I thought, as I looked at his chiseled face.

"I know that those of you that are here today have experienced the nine truths. I know that your lives have drastically changed and have moved forward in a direction you never thought imaginable. This moment right here, right now, is exactly where you belong.

"Like the others, you were skeptical, but you had the cognitive capability of seeing past your skepticism and fear and eventually grew neutral to the magical process that synchronized before your very eyes. Allow me to congratulate you for getting through the past week! I am truly proud of you!"

Brian started to clap his hands loudly and then he put two fingers in his mouth and whistled a loud screeching cheer. As he did that, Diana joined his clapping and so did I. The rest of the class chimed in as well, and there, in the midst of the grassy knoll of Braxton College, a group of spiritually enlightened students clapped and rejoiced victoriously in our accomplishment. The wealth of knowledge that we received was unparalleled to anything that we had experienced before, and the entire class of students stood up tall, and gave ourselves a standing ovation. Dr. Jacobs was beaming brightly, as he clapped and cheered in our triumph. He was thrilled for us, and I felt grateful for the cosmic coincidence that led me to his class of philosophical wisdom. The cheering slowly subsided as we saw that Dr. Jacobs was ready to address the class again.

"Now that we are all filled with energy and feel the love of the universe, I would like you all to try to relive the experience that you had from directly after the first class, right up to this moment. In order to do this completely you must clear your mind completely. Do not think of anything. Concentrate on the word 'nothing.' Try not to let any thoughts go through your head. This could take about ten minutes for you to get into a clear mind state."

I closed my eyes for a moment and felt the sun on my face.

"I am not here. Do no think of what you need to do after this class, do not think of what happened this morning, do not think about the

ON THE STRINGS OF VIOLINS

fact that you forgot to take out the garbage, or the other homework you may have; none of that matters in this moment. Just concentrate on nothingness. Nothing, nothing, nothing. Clear your mind. Clear, clear, clear."

His voice was soft and soothing. It penetrated my skin and I felt calm and relaxed. It was hard to think of nothing, but I was desperately trying to become energized and feel love enough to clear my mind. That was, in fact, the key to everything. If I could tap into the love around me I knew I could accomplish anything I wanted to. Nathan taught me about this truth, and it was my favorite one of all. I thought about the experiment we had about the forces of energy and the word "time."

However, now I was supposed to think of nothing and just clear my mind. I sat with my eyes closed and tried to become clear. Thoughts raced through my mind, and I allowed myself to feel the thoughts, surrender to them, and then let them go. As I did this and kept repeating the process, the thoughts started to slow down. They didn't come to mind as rapidly. The key was to feel the love of the universe, breathe in and breathe out, and when a thought came to mind, I fully felt that thought, then surrendered to it and let it go. The more I did this, the less thoughts would enter, and the clearer I became. I breathed in and out, and felt completely relaxed and secure. I was full of energy and complete power.

The energy of the students doing the same thing was invigorating. I could feel all their energy pulsating, and the energy of the sun, the trees, the sky, the grass, the land, and all their living energy was one with mine. In fact, the power of this great energy of the universe acting together intensified my own energy level and became the energy level of the whole, or the entire universe. This feeling was like no other. I had felt full of life before, but nothing compared to this feeling. The energy level of forty students combined with the energy of the universe was euphoric. I could feel the energy of the entire universe times forty.

My eyes still closed, sitting still, my entire body became as light as a feather and began to tingle with numbness. I felt like I was floating on

153

air. I no longer felt as if my body was touching the ground. I was being engulfed by the enormous energy we created, and it was the most comforting and enjoyable feeling I had ever known. At that point, the thoughts were coming to mind less and less and almost stopped altogether, except for the occasional thought that would find its way in. With my eyes closed, breathing deeply, I concentrated harder.

Dr. Jacobs' soothing voice was heard again. "Reflect upon the coincidence that led you to my class. I'm sure it was a twist of fate that brought you here. Think about it and relive it in your mind."

I was taken back three weeks ago when I first found out from my advisor that I had to take another philosophy class to fulfill my major. I was so upset when she told me. I looked at it as a setback, as another hellish obstacle that I had to overcome in my path to graduating. My mind took me back to that fateful day.

I was sitting on the couch in the apartment leafing through the class schedule booklet to enroll in my classes. I remember feeling so mad and so anxious about choosing the proper schedule for myself. If I had to take a philosophy class, originally, I wanted to take Dr. Tillman's class that was held at eleven-thirty. I wanted to take Dr. Tillman's course because I had taken him before and I thought his class would be easy. I wanted to breeze through it so that I could concentrate more on my journalism classes. But Dr. Tillman's class was filled. At the time, I was really upset. The only other choice I had was taking the early class held by Dr. Jacobs. I thought that taking such an early class would screw everything up. I'd never make it to the class on time. I had never heard of Dr. Jacobs, and I didn't know anyone in the class. I usually never took a class unless a friend was also taking it. I was scared and skeptical because I didn't know how challenging his class would be. Before, I always looked for the easiest way out. I always looked for a way that would benefit me so that I didn't have to change my beliefs or attitudes about what I expected.

Now I could see that taking Jacobs' class was the best thing. It was no accident I ended up in this class; it was meant to be.

ON THE STRINGS OF VIOLINS

"Can you feel how you felt at the time? Surrender yourself to that feeling, and let it go." As he said this, I saw that situation unfolding before my very eyes, like I was watching a movie of myself enrolling in the class. I saw myself calling and enrolling in the automated system. I had an angry expression on my face, and I could feel the angst that my mind and body were going through at that moment. I felt so uncertain about it, as my angry fingers pushed the course schedule numbers into the automated system. A look of rage was in my eyes and my body was burning inside.

Sitting there at that moment on the grassy knoll, I felt that experience fully, then surrendered myself to it and let it go. I knew that all the other students had similar situations they were watching being played out in their minds. They replayed the coincidental happenings that brought them to this class, and I could feel their uncertainty at that time as well. They were slowly letting go of their old feelings, and were rejoicing in their serendipitous fate. I could feel their energy rise as mine rose with them. It was as if a ton of weight had been lifted off our chests and we could breathe lightly again.

"You may open your eyes now," Dr. Jacobs spoke calmly. Like a butterfly's wings, my eyes fluttered open and tried to focus. As my focus became clearer, I looked at Dr. Jacobs and saw him standing holding an old shiny violin. He held the violin by the neck in his left hand and the bow in his other hand. I looked at Brian and Diana with a puzzled expression as they looked back at me.

"Now that you all realize that it was your destiny to experience these truths, you must learn how to keep these truths in you consciousness at all times so they can manifest and grow with you as you evolve into the future. By keeping them alive in your consciousness you are awakening your sense of what our life is really about. It's about recognizing that we are on this plane to learn and to evolve together, and that we can accomplish monumental things if we function as a whole unit. We can raise our vibrational level higher and higher. Let me show you how this is done."

Dr. Jacobs lifted up his shiny violin and projected it outward toward the class. As he raised his fiddle the sun's light danced on the sheen of the violin and the glare sparkled deep into my eyes. We inched closer to him with our mouths open and our ears in tune. Dr. Jacobs' face was filled with excitement.

"I want you to imagine that each one of you is a string on this violin. Each string has its own complexity, its own depth, its own characteristic, its own richness, its own sound, its own tone, its own voice." I marveled at the strings on his violin and noticed how they were perfectly created to produce its desired sound. Some were thicker, some thinner, some tighter, some looser, some more precise, some more lax. As the professor held the violin up in the air, my eyes immediately went to the third string from the top. For some reason, I was drawn to that one and I examined it fully.

"I want each of you to look at the violin and pick a string that symbolizes you." Dr. Jacobs said. Since I had already picked my string, I turned to look at Brian and Diana. They looked at their string with wonderment.

"Now that you have picked your string, I want you to focus on your surroundings and fill yourselves with energy." I looked at the big oak trees in the distance and the evergreens around me. I looked up at the sky and the cottony white clouds. I felt the rich thick green grass that I was sitting on. I focused on their beauty and how each of these parts of the earth are also a part of me. My chest began to fill with air as a feeling of euphoria ran through me. I could feel the energy levels of Brian and Diana increasing as well as the other students around me. Their energy was feeding me as mine was feeding theirs. It was magnificent.

"What I will do now is play each string individually. I want you to concentrate and focus deeply on the string's level of vibration as it passes through all the different energy fields. Keep in mind that the faster the string vibrates, the higher the pitch, and the lower the string vibrates, the lower the pitch of the sound. Concentrate on the way the string's energy and vibration penetrates your mind and body. I want you to

156

center yourself on the level of vibration and feel it in your core. First, I will start out with the lower pitch strings. Are you all ready?"

He looked at the class of forty-plus students sitting on the grass. He had our complete attention. "I said, are you ready?" He said it louder as we all looked at him and nodded. Dr. Jacobs cleared his throat and swallowed. His feet moved slightly. He raised the bow and put the violin under the left side of his chin. You could hear a pin drop as everyone sat in anticipation.

Dr. Jacobs played the sound of the first string. The low vibrating tone was instantly absorbed by my ears as the sound of the tone jumped off the violin. The sound was slowly moving as it inched closer and closer to me. I allowed it to penetrate my skin as it slowly moved deeper and deeper into my soul. As the sound continued its pulsating vibration, Dr. Jacobs said, "I want those of you that picked this string as a symbol of yourself to identify with this sound and realize that you are an important part of the entire scale, and that you are a vital contributor to this particular vibrational scale that you exist upon." I could feel the energy of those students that picked this string and as the tone played they became a part of it and the euphoria of the whole group became even more intense.

Dr. Jacobs then played the next string on the violin. This string had a slightly higher vibrational energy as it danced into our ears and sang into our beings. I could feel the enthusiasm and the love of the class grow even higher as I recognized the students who picked that string to identify with. My energy had risen to an even higher state; I felt lighter and my mind became clearer.

At last Dr. Jacobs played the string I had picked to identify me. As soon as he strummed the bow over my string, I immediately recognized the sound. It was a sound that seemed so familiar to me, like it had been singing inside of me all along. It was the most beautiful tone I had known. It was my tone and its song has always been playing in my core. The level of vibration was the level at which I had always been vibrating. In a way, that string was me. It was magical and enlightening. My energy became even more intensified as I realized this discovery. This

157

tone was the tone of knowledge and beauty and wisdom beyond the levels of anything on this earthly plane. This song has been a part of me from heaven. Diana and Brian gazed over at me and saw me becoming full of light.

Dr. Jacobs played all the other strings until the entire class had heard their own vibrational sound. Each of us was filled with their own energy and the energy of the entire group. I felt as light as a cloud. The complete euphoria I felt was indescribable. Dr. Jacobs stopped playing and put down the violin for a moment. He studied us, and seemed pleased at what he saw.

"I can feel that you fully recognized your own string and your own vibration. Now you have discovered that we are all operating at a special vibration. But the question is why? The answer is quite simple. Individually, we can do great things, but as a whole unit together we can raise our levels of energy to a new level."

I looked at Brian and Diana as they gazed back at me. "Now, I want you to remember your string's vibration. But this time, I am going to play the strings all together. I want you to understand how electric these sounds and vibrations are when they move in synchronistic unison. When I strike the strings together their vibrations will multiply and the sounds will move in harmony as if they were always meant to be heard, appreciated, and admired this way. I also want you to recognize the importance of the bow that is strumming the strings to move in a particular direction. I want you to remember that the bow is like the outside factors of life that force us to move in one direction or the other. The bow is the catalyst that makes the strings move together or apart. The bow is that twist of fate. It's like the coincidences that help us."

Dr. Jacobs raised his bow high in the air. The class gasped in anticipation. We knew that with one strum of the violin each one of us would hear our own tone played simultaneously with everyone else's tone. Dr. Jacobs looked at the class. Our energy was as high as heaven. My face was numb. I was on pins and needles. Dr. Jacobs' bow strummed the strings together playing the most beautiful sound I had ever heard. I heard my tone being played with the tones of Brian and Diana and the

ON THE STRINGS OF VIOLINS

other students in the class. It was surreal. As the notes played our spirits were free and alive. I was exhilarated to the very depth of my being. I could feel of the love of everyone in the class, the universe of the sky, the land, the sun, the trees, the lakes, the rivers, the clouds, the grass, and everything that was alive and breathing. I looked at my surrounding amidst the grassy knoll as every living thing was pulsating and moving in synchronicity. As nature moves in synchronicity, so do our bodies, and so do our lives.

Dr. Jacobs looked at the class. "This life is your symphony. The music has always been with you, but now you are ready to truly hear it. Recognize it, nourish it, and rejoice in it. We are one. We are one," he exalted.

I was truly thankful for this class, for the past week, for Brian, Diana, our guides along the way, the Plague, Jeff Greenberg, the baseball players, and for Nathan. But most importantly, I was grateful for listening to my philosophical symphony. I knew now that this symphony would always pulsate through me.

The best use of life
is to invest it in something that will outlast life.
—William James

XIII

A DEEPER ASSIGNMENT

Dr. Jacobs observed the class. He put down the violin. "Now that you have learned the nine truths of life and have heard your own music, it is time to understand where we as a culture are headed. The remainder of the class will be to reiterate these truths into our daily lives. Our daily lives must be fused into our ongoing culture. But first, you must fully understand the philosophy of the previous eras.

"Everyone on this great earth is growing in terms of our spiritual awareness. The Material Age is coming to an end and the Information Age is beginning. Signs of the Information Age have already presented themselves with the onset of great technological advancements. However, the technological advancements are only the beginning of this era, which will consist of becoming truly spiritual in a divine manner. The higher form of spirituality will be found by exchanging spiritual information with others. The power of informational advancements will be more profound than any monetary advancement." Dr. Jacobs was making complete sense to me as he spoke. I took notes as fast as I could.

"The great Material Age has endured for four hundred years, supplying the world with all of the necessities to live comfortably. The next step is to realize why we went through this era. We did this to reach the Information Age, which has already begun. By the time we reach the middle of the Information Age, the world will consist of highly spiritual and intellectual people gaining spiritual information about the world and most importantly about ourselves. People will live at a higher level of vibrational energy and will be happier and more fulfilled than ever before. In order to understand this shift of thought, you must revert your thinking to your knowledge of history and the various thought processes throughout civilization.

"In the Dark Ages around the year 1,000 BC, individuals were either working class or nobility. Their lives revolved around the church and the teaching of churchmen. The churchmen held supreme power over the people because they verified if a person was acting in a godly manner, or if they were succumbing to the temptations of the devil.

"At that time, people's spirituality was demonstrated by adhering to the laws of the church. Civilization's thought process was very simple. People thought that "truth" was simply obeying the words of the scriptures and that by doing so they would be rewarded by entering the kingdom of heaven. However, by the 1,600s, people started to get wise to the churchmen and their corrupt ways of government. They thought, why should we listen to the churchmen if they are not acting in a godly and just manner themselves? The churchmen were manipulating their power over others to gain personal wealth and prosperity. Nonetheless, people started to revolt against the power of the church. Thus, Martin Luther and the other leaders of the world started to contemplate higher ideas of a more supreme form of spirituality.

"Many religions were created to break away from the corrupt churchmen. In addition, Galileo and other astronomers discovered the sun did not revolve around the earth. The earth was merely one small planet amidst millions of stars and other galaxies. This was a very frightening discovery because people recognized that the earth was no longer the center of the universe. Everything that civilization held as true, was no longer; thus, arose many questions that required explanation.

"From that point on, the worldview took a drastic turn. Explorers set sail to new lands with the scientific method approach and attempted to find answers. However, something happened along the way. As the explorers and adventurers settled onto new lands, they found that their questions took longer to answer than they anticipated. They encountered new opportunities, and took advantage of the vast resources of the earth. They occupied themselves with obtaining security, safety, and comfort in the New World. They started building, creating, inventing, and obtaining financial wealth. Thus, they distanced themselves from the true meaning of what they had set out to accomplish. In essence, they became distracted and preoccupied by obtaining wealth and security in the vast New World, and abandoned the reason they settled there in the first place. The answers they were looking for became secondary to obtaining security and wealth. The Material Age had begun. The questions the early settlers abandoned are still left unanswered.

"For the past four hundred years, we have been using all the resources of Earth and preoccupying ourselves with a sense of safety and security. We have revolved our lives around our work or occupation as a way of avoiding the question, 'What's this life for?'

"Now, we have built a world in which all the comforts of life can be produced. However, because of our focused, driven need to create comfort and security, we leave the resources of our planet polluted and on the verge of devastation. We are clearly reaching a climax in our cultural direction. Now, we find ourselves at a crossroads, or turning point of heightened spiritual alertness and awareness. Because of the terrorist attacks and the conflicts in the Middle East, our sense of safety and security has diminished. Is the universe trying to tell us something?

"Throughout the Material Age we have been obsessed with obtaining all the comforts of the world. We have been using our professions and our monetary achievements as the sole indicators of self-validation. We have succeeded. The Material Age in which we live is slowly entering the Information Age, an age in which knowledge will be viewed as more valuable than any material gain or possession. We are now ready to discover how to enter this new age, and what the next step toward our spiritual path on earth is." The class leaned forward eagerly as Dr. Jacobs proceeded.

"The assignment for your next class is to go on a scavenger hunt. This scavenger hunt will help you incorporate the nine truths into your daily lives. On my website there will be a new clue posted every day, and you will have to go to the appropriate place here on campus to discover what this clue is. All the clues have to do with the knowledge you've already learned. You and your partners might have to travel off campus to learn about the clues. Believe me, this will be a very enlightening experience. Look on my website tomorrow morning for the first clue. Good luck and have fun."

Dr. Jacobs gathered his belongings and walked into the sun. And there in the midst of the campus quadrangle we were full of infinite possibilities.

ABOUT THE AUTHOR

Ann Marie Zakos has a bachelor's degree in communications from DePaul University. She resides in Chicago.

Give the Gift of

FIRST CLASS TICKET
—A NOVEL—
to Your Friends and Colleagues

CHECK YOUR LEADING BOOKSTORE OR ORDER HERE

❑ **YES**, I want _____ copies of *First Class Ticket* at $14.95 each, plus $4.95 shipping per book (Illinois residents please add $1.01 sales tax per book). Canadian orders must be accompanied by a postal money order in U.S. funds. Allow 15 days for delivery.

My check or money order for $_____ is enclosed.

Please charge my: ❑ Visa ❑ MasterCard
❑ Discover ❑ American Express

Name _____

Organization _____

Address _____

City/State/Zip _____

Phone_____ E-mail _____

Card # _____

Exp. Date_____ Signature _____

Please make your check payable and return to:
Magnum Veritas Publishing
P.O. Box 355
Elk Grove Village, IL 60009
Call your credit card order to: (866) 766-7404
Fax: (630) 766-7402 www.annmariezakos.com